Rebellious Britain:
Power Cut 2023

Colin Walpole

First published in the United Kingdom in 2024
by The Choir Press

ISBN 978-1-78963-498-3

By the same author
A World without Money or Politicians
The Lives and Deaths of Terry Toft
Experimenting with Short Stories
Rosie's Fear
Mr Tolly of Greenwich Park
Alfege, Greenwich and the Mystic Eggs
Kerb Drill and Other Short Stories

The author reserves the right to offend.

Dedication

To the author's uncle Leslie George Weir, who was killed in action at nineteen years of age on 12 December 1944. The young flight engineer's Lancaster bomber was shot down over Germany during a bombing raid in the Second World War.

Georgie rests in Durnbach War Cemetery, 45 kilometres south of Munich.

Contents

Introduction: Grounds for Revolution   vi

Part One   1

Removing the Capital from Capitalism   2

The Inaugural People's Parliament, 4 January 2023   31

Northern Ireland   52

Checks and Balances   54

The Second Parliament, 18 January 2023, 10 a.m.   55

The Heist   61

Part Two   75

Day Zero – The Albert Pub, 18 January 2023, 7 p.m.   76

Julia   77

The Stepladder   88

Gemma and Oscar   98

George   101

Fielding, Mullard and Davies   104

Lucy and Nicola   114

Conclusion   122

Timeline   124

Introduction:
Grounds for Revolution

The old boys drinking in the Royal Albert weren't revolting – at least they didn't think so. They were just old friends who had known each other since their teenage years in the 1960s and who would carry on drinking until that final 'drink up gentlemen, please,' ushered them into the next world and teetotal eternity.

But revolution was in the air.

The revolution would be approved or rejected on 18 January 2023. It would be the men, women and children of Britain who would decide – not politicians. Observers around the world watched.

Things have to be pretty dire for the British people to revolt. So, what pushed them to brink? Those living in the UK for the past thirty or forty years need no clues to that question. For those from further afield: the behaviour of key political figures – chaos at Westminster – unbridled immigration – representative democracy – the unfair distribution of wealth – crime – and global warming; for starters!

The crux of the matter was 'the system' – the way the country is run – the way the world is run. It was dawning on many, that we as a species would have to change the way we manage our affairs, otherwise there would be no planet capable of sustaining life.

Back in the Royal Albert in Greenwich, South East London, the old chaps supped their beer unaware of the approaching tsunami.

Part One

Removing the Capital from Capitalism

The Royal Albert public house in South East London had been the regular watering hole of a group of friends back in the 1960s and '70s. Life's more enduring responsibilities – families and careers – imposed an inconvenient fifty-year pause to their drinking routine; and now in the late summer of 2022, in the autumn of their lives they made up for lost time. They reminisced and exchanged news. The same old jokes were laughed at as if they were brand new. They tossed around current affairs as they used to toss a rugby ball along the line – and politicians were often kicked into the long grass, too. Lads no more, the conversation leaned more towards lumbago and prostate than girls and parties.

The alfa imbiber was Harry Sparrow or Aristotle as he was known (hardly anyone was called by the names on their birth certificates) and a nickname might last forever or just for that evening. So, because he was a bit philosophical, the 'H' in Harry was dropped, as they often are in this part of the world, and 'Arry morphed to Aristotle. Aristotle was a retired welder and well-chosen words flew like the white sparks ricocheting off his blackened workshop floor.

Then there was Fish, the one-eyed postman, he'd lost an eye while mackerel fishing off the Devon coast. He'd also lost most of the index finger of his right hand to a dog while posting a letter. He had previously been known as Captain Birdseye from the advert. That changed briefly to Captain Careless when he lost his finger, Fish Finger came next, and that was shortened to Fish.

Fish had been jailed for six years for a crime he hadn't committed. His wife had been murdered and because he discovered the body, and was covered in her blood he became the prime suspect. Years later, forensic evidence proved the murder to be the work of a prolific serial killer. Fish was cleared of the crime, released and compensated but he never recovered from the double trauma.

Stick used to have a proper name back in the day, and was known for years as Lofty. The transition from a tall, upright rugby player to the stooping old man was gradual, as you would imagine, his decline reached a significant milestone when he arrived at the pub sporting a walking stick.

The name Lofty changed first to Walking Stick and that was quickly shortened to Stick. Sciatica slowed his walk to a shuffle and his stick named him as well as steadying him.

Baldy was younger, in his late forties. He sported a fine head of blond hair which could hang in ringlets or be tied in a ponytail depending on his mood. Baldy had never married and to compensate had an imaginary girlfriend, Daphne. He'd never had a proper job and lived with his mother for whom he was a registered carer. Tattoos and body piercings linked him to a younger generation but he preferred the company of his older mates.

Lordy was the pub landlord; he and his wife lived above the Royal Albert. Lordy was the father figure; he was streetwise, diplomatic and understood people and their foibles. There was a time when owning a pub used to be a profitable business; folk were carefree in those days, the long-term effects of decades of unbridled alcohol consumption weren't so well known. And now, in 2022, the pub was losing money and Lordy didn't know how much longer he could hold out before the bailiffs came knocking.

They were an unremarkable bunch of politically incorrect, straight-talking South-East Londoners.

In the weeks and months ahead, events would conspire to expand the group to assimilate new friends from the city.

But this evening was tinged with sadness, it wasn't known if the Queen would make it through the night. Even the anti-royalists among them had a fondness for the Queen. The telly above the bar switched between Buckingham Palace, Balmoral and Liz Truss, the new prime minister swanking her way through the door of Number 10. Sadness squared.

*

Baldy: 'Who's coming shopping?'

Stick: 'Not me, I'm too slow and if we 'ave to do a runner I'll get caught. I'll stay here and keep Lordy company. Swipe me a couple of tins of corned beef.'

Baldy: 'I'll put it on my list. How many "customers" do you reckon there'll be?'

Stick: 'About eighty, could be more. There's transport laid on at the Barley Mow and the Tolly; word gets around.'

The pub emptied and two awaiting minibuses filled up. This wasn't uncouth looting; there were rules of conduct, no booze or tobacco. The employees at the supermarket were complicit and it was all very chummy, certainly no violence or smashing of windows.

The checkout assistants sat passively as the 'customers' helped themselves to plastic bags, filled them and left without paying.

The police were called. None responded.

Neither the police nor the legal system could cope any more. The government had lost it. Britain had become ungovernable. Displays of civil disobedience were increasing; many people weren't paying their rent, mortgages or utility bills. For many, *civil disobedience* didn't come into the reckoning – they simply couldn't afford to pay the bills – they didn't have the money.

Revolutionary change was called for; a political shift from right wing to left wing wasn't enough. Sacking the Tories wasn't enough, the political system – including the economic model had to be stripped out and replaced by new systems. An infrastructure with a wider power base and a purer form of democracy was on the agenda.

Two core principles were central to the rebellion: 'direct democracy' and a 'moneyless economy'. Policies and law would be decided by the people – all the people. The new regime wasn't a political party – not in the accepted sense. This meant that it had neither the structure nor the ideology to fight in a general election. The revolutionary movement rejected flag-waving, power-seeking personalities. Sound ideas sourced through robust debate were preferred to Churchillian oration or dictatorial passion.

Instead of traditional politics, an app is available to all, where policy and law are debated. Power is in the hands of the entire population of the UK and ultimately the people decide on a case-by-case basis. Complex and difficult matters would be explored using the existing practice of 'citizens' assemblies'. These consist of a jury of about three hundred randomly selected people who together with experts debate the issue. It may take several days to thoroughly thrash out a subject and the findings would be broadcast and voted for or against, online. Where necessary several such assemblies would be held around the country simultaneously, so as to search out the correct solution.

Citizens' assemblies would emerge as a crucial tool in the running of the country. Specialists would provide the facts and the people or jury would apply the common sense.

'Should we go to war?' 'Should music be taught in our schools?' 'How do we prevent raw sewage entering our rivers?' Everyone is then able to contribute to the debate and those responsible for voting (detailed later) would vote. No longer would it be those with financial interests who would persuade at the House of Commons. The process would explore all avenues until a fitting solution or compromise was found. But no more playing politics, it was clear to all that politics and the vulgar circus of highly paid commentators and journalists was not fit for purpose. The entertaining sideshow would have to be withdrawn. The parlour game consisting of teams telling intricate sets of lies no longer amused.

Under the new regime there will be no such games.

The removal of money would prove more contentious than sacking politicians. Balanced argument would convince many that a change away from the existing political model was due. However, the advantages of a moneyless economy are not so immediately obvious – completely alien more to the point. The rationale behind the argument to remove money from the economy came not only from established socialist groups; wealthy individuals from the city were coming full circle … a millionaire trader called Lee would soon find his way to the Royal Albert pub.

*

Lordy addressed his only remaining customer: 'Are you ready for another pint, Stick?'

Stick gave the thumbs-up and Lordy joined him. 'So, you didn't fancy a bit of semi-illegal shoplifting?'

'Nah, too much aggro, and if we had to do a runner I'd slow 'em down. I must admit though, I don't know where this will lead.'

'Civil disobedience they call it,' said Lordy. 'I think it's all right as long as it remains peaceful. There's nothing wrong with the ordinary bloke in the street standing up for himself. Those city traders in Canary Wharf, walking off with millions in bonuses while mothers can't feed the kids or pay the rent, it's disgusting.'

'But what's the point? Civil disobedience ain't gonna change nothing.'

'You'd be surprised,' said Lordy. 'They reckon they're gonna get rid of money.'

Stick laughed, 'Yeah, I heard that, it'll never work, you can't live without money. You can't keep on nicking stuff from the supermarket, they'll close 'em down. What will happen then? No food.'

Lordy: 'It's all about being organised. The scale of it will be nationwide. As long as the farmers produce the food we shouldn't see a significant change.'

Stick: 'And who's going to pay the farmers? And where's the diesel coming from to shunt the meat and veg to the markets? This ain't been properly thought through. And who is in charge, Robin Hood?'

Lordy: 'Well it ain't me; there's no particular person in charge. Listen, ordinary people ask questions on an app, they contribute ideas and solutions to problems – and you've got a point – where does the diesel come from? That could be a question worth asking.'

Stick: 'How do you mean? Ask a question? Ask who?'

Lordy: 'Ask everyone. Online, it all happens online, an app on your mobile.'

Stick: 'I ain't got a mobile phone.'

'Oh, of course you haven't.' Lordy thought for a bit and tapped away at his phone, speaking each word so that Stick could follow. 'Where does the fuel come from to transport foodstuffs around the country? Who pays for the imported diesel?' He left the phone on the table and fetched a couple of bags of crisps. The phone vibrated, he read; 'The pound sterling will be backed by the nation's gold reserves and secured by the Treasury for foreign trade. It is planned to reorganise agriculture into local areas to keep transport to a minimum and for transport to convert gradually to electric vehicles. Meanwhile the Bank of England will pay for imported fuels.'

Stick: 'Who's answering the questions? Who's pulling the strings – and what's in it for them?'

Lordy: 'There's no *one* person answering the questions, it's everyone in the system. So, if you register on the app you can ask questions and respond to other people's questions. Let me give you an example. Say you are a vegetarian and think that killing animals and eating meat should be outlawed; you register your suggestion and everyone else has the opportunity to comment.'

Stick: 'That's a bit extreme isn't it?'

Lordy: 'Yeah but you get the point. There will be freedom of speech and nothing is taboo. Someone might think the traffic lights at the end of the road should be replaced by a roundabout, or the local school should have more playing fields. Anything goes, it's proper democracy – direct democracy, it's not going cap in hand to the government or council who will look at budgets and give it a first, second and third reading before kicking into touch. There are no budgets – because there will be no money. If a majority of the local voters says yes to more playing fields then it will be planned – all the detail, the where and how – and the project will be launched just as it is today.'

Stick: 'And who's paying for it? That's what I want to know. The gardeners, knocking down buildings, levelling the ground, it don't come cheap.'

Lordy: 'I know it's not easy to picture. I suppose a project leader plans the new playing fields, the school is consulted and the neighbours. too, then when everything is ready, the experts come and do the job. And no money changes hands, no backhanders to get the contract. The landscapers arrive and start measuring up for the new cricket pitch and the project gets completed. Less stressful for the workers I would imagine. There is no money, there are no wages, everything is free – it will be just like tonight with all the 'Erberts nicking groceries from the supermarket – but it won't be stealing; they will be doing it legally. Everything carries on, people go to work, and the kids go to school.'

Stick: 'But no one gets paid.'

Lordy: 'No, there's no money. You won't need money.'

Stick: 'That's gonna piss off the bankers …'

Lordy: '… and the traders and hedge fund managers, but bear in mind they can protest on the app that "the no-money policy" is grossly unfair on them, and that they won't get their hundred-grand bonuses.'

Stick: 'Ha ha, I like it. But it means no stock exchange, what about pension funds?'

Lordy: 'Gone – no need.'

Stick: 'But when will it happen?'

Lordy: 'Good question. At the moment there are about twenty

million people registered in the system, the UK has a population of around sixty-seven million. For the movement to be taken seriously, it's thought that it'll need 80 or 90 per cent before the people are free to run Britain.'

Stick: 'Sixty-seven million, does that include kids?'

Lordy: 'Yeah, and if little four-year-old Mary demands more ice cream it'll be the same as Mr Trader demanding his bonuses back.'

Stick: 'Ha ha, but what will happen with the police, and the armed forces, the justice system, the courts and all that?'

Lordy: 'It's reckoned that many of the top people in these groups have registered, so it's only a matter of time. They may only be curious but that's okay. They need to know what's happening, and it's a good thing they're in the mix. They are a brainy bunch and the country needs brains.'

Stick: 'When did all this kick off? Why haven't I heard of it before?'

Lordy: 'Well, if you ain't got a smartphone, you're at a disadvantage. But you can register on mine.'

Stick: 'My missis would 'ave loved this, hated those Tories she did. I'll register on your phone if that's all right with you.'

*

8 September 2022

The following evening Stick and his mates sat in the corner discussing the Queen's death which had just been announced. The pub was quiet for a Thursday evening. Many families were gathered around the telly and dabbing their eyes.

Baldy stayed at home comforting his mum. She watched the coverage while Baldy made a cup of tea.

Mum: 'Aren't you seeing Daphne tonight? You see her every night.'

Baldy: 'Nah, she was a bit upset and wanted a quiet night in to reflect, you know. Here's your tea, Mum, and I bought a nice Victoria sponge.' He joined her in front of the television.

Mum: 'Why don't you ask Daphne round here for the Queen's funeral … it would be nice to meet her.'

Baldy washed down a mouthful of Victoria sponge, 'Yeah, all right, I'll ask her.'

'You always say that but she never comes.'

'I'm thinking of chucking her anyway, she talks too much and there's someone else after me …'

'Ooh, you are a one …'

*

Stick had splashed out on a smartphone and his mates proffered well-meaning advice. 'You lot are confusing me. Lordy is good at explaining things. I'll ask him.' He moved to a bar stool.

Lordy: 'Can you see the screen? It seems like you can't see the screen.'

Stick: 'Of course I can see the screen.'

'Can you read what it says?'

'Yeah, no, well if I hold it at arm's length.' He demonstrated.

'What does it say?'

'I dunno, I can't read it.' He stuffed it irreverently in his pocket without closing it down. 'Look, I've got a bit of a situation at home; well not my home … it's my son and daughter-in-law. They are about to have their house repossessed and I wondered if that new system could help in any way. He lost his job during Covid and her cleaning jobs don't pay enough, even under normal circumstances it would be tight, but with prices rocketing through the roof …'

'Let me think,' Lordy massaged his face wearily as if he'd been up all night. 'I'll have a word with a bloke I know, leave it with me. Membership has grown to thirty million since yesterday.'

Stick: 'What! Grown from twenty to thirty million overnight?'

Lordy: 'Yeah, amazing, eh? But that expansion is causing some problems, the program hardware is not coping and they're bolting on some additional memory.'

Stick: 'I'm envious.'

Lordy: 'There is so much duplicated messaging – there is a word recognition system which needs improving. But the good news is that more talent from the city is signing up to the app.'

Stick: 'How is that good news?'

Lordy: 'They're not all bad, and we need them on our side. Their understanding of money is quite different to ours. Most of us have learned about money by not 'aving any. They are establishing a new bank.'

Stick: 'I thought we had enough banks ... and how can someone start up a new bank? We're not talking about a corner shop. And what's the point of another bank if there's gonna be no money?'

Lordy: 'There might be no point at all. Look, what we're facing here is massive, an epic change in life as we know it. If the revolution is voted through, life in Britain will be very different, but if it fails, or if success comes slowly – no one knows what dirty tricks the Tory government has up its sleeve – there needs to be contingency plans. That's why the new bank is necessary – to help people in your son's situation.

'The bank is planning to buy up property under threat of repossession, just like your son's, and then leasing it back at peppercorn rent. At some stage, in a few months perhaps – if the body of support continues rising at this pace – money in its traditional sense will not exist.'

Stick: 'I'm not sure I trust these city folk.'

Lordy looked at his phone, 'Thirty-one million. It's going mad. The new bank might not have to intervene – there won't be time. When the British people run Britain – and I've a feeling it won't be long now – there won't be "house prices" there will be homes, where people live, keep warm and drink tea. Don't worry. Leave this with me. I'll get Lee to come and 'ave a chat with you on how to start your own bank.'

Stick: 'Not really an ambition of mine, but it would be interesting to know. And who is Lee?'

Lordy: 'He's a former trader, money coming out of his ears; he scored big bonuses in his day, but an okay bloke who has turned his back on that lifestyle.' Lordy returned to pulling pints.

*

Lee joined Stick and his mates. They were disarmed by Lee's 'cor blimey' accent. Most of the city traders they'd seen on television were silver-spoon-sucking rich kids fresh out of university. Lee sounded as if he hadn't seen the inside of a primary school.

Lee: 'There needs to be a group of you to fill all the various roles – oh, and five million quid. You need to be clean – no criminal record, a background in finance and approved by the various authorities. Providing you fit the profile, it's quite straightforward. Who is thinking of going into banking? It takes a bit of time to set up and this ain't the best environment considering the anticipated downfall of money.'

Lee was a mathematics genius from working-class stock. His uncluttered mind and clear thinking had shot him to prominence and 'top trader' three years on the trot. But his working-class roots eventually made it impossible for him to accept such a ridiculous level of easy wealth. Lee was influential in setting up the app.

Stick: 'It was just out of interest, excuse the pun, Lordy was saying that some traders were putting together a new bank in case the revolution drags on.'

Lee: 'Yeah, that's right. A big bail-out campaign is planned to prevent repossessions.'

Fish: 'But five million ain't a lot. With house prices around here that's about ten houses.'

Lee: 'Ah, that's not how it works. For a start it's expected that supporters of the new system are ready to transfer some pretty serious money into the new bank. And then, I don't know the extent of your financial understanding, but banks are permitted to lend more money than they hold, ten times more in fact; it's called fractional reserve banking.'

Fish: 'What? How does that work? It sounds like a Ponzi scheme to me.'

Stick: 'What's a Ponzi scheme?'

Aristotle: 'One of those pyramid money-making schemes. Steer well clear of 'em.'

Lee: 'It is a bit and it's nothing new, similar practices began under the "gold standard" regime. Problems only arise if there's a bank run when all the depositors demand their cash.'

'Like in the 1946 film *It's a Wonderful Life* starring James Stewart,' said Aristotle.

Lee: 'Precisely.'

'And that's allowed,' said Fish, 'a bank can lend money it doesn't have?'

'It ain't right,' said Lordy.

Fish: 'It's scandalous.'

'I agree,' said Lee, 'I totally agree and that's why many economists, traders and bankers are behind the revolution.'

'Why should we trust these city people?' said Fish. 'What makes them suddenly so benevolent?'

Lee: 'Without their know-how, the revolution wouldn't stand a chance of succeeding. It's widely accepted that capitalism is no longer sustainable. Britain isn't the only country with problems. The rich own the media and the media tells us what to think. Liz Truss tells us that "growth" is the answer – nothing new there – but when does the growth stop? Industry is producing shit we don't need. Advertisers tell us we need shit. And we are stupid enough to go out and buy shit. The shit ends up on the beaches of the world because it's mainly plastic shit.'

Fish: 'You say capitalism isn't sustainable – that's a bit of a sweeping statement. Who says so and why?'

Lee: 'Blimey, there's no flies on you lot! Capitalism has been okay, there's no getting away from that. But over the past forty to fifty years there has been a massive change in the way the world functions. Computers, the Internet, robots and artificial intelligence ...'

Baldy enters the pub to a round of applause and laughter.

Lordy: 'Perfect timing, Baldy, we were just talking about artificial intelligence. What you 'aving, the usual?'

Fish: 'I thought you were round Daphne's tonight.'

Baldy: 'Yeah, she wanted an early night, headache or something, you know what they're like.'

Lordy: 'This is Lee; he was telling us about robots and money. Carry on Lee – this is Baldy by the way.'

Lee: 'Yeah, so capitalism needs consumers to make it work. People consume and robots don't – people can only consume if they have money, obviously – and because of automation there are fewer jobs, so that source of money is shrinking. Are you with me? Consuming includes bread and butter but also cars, clothes and holidays; anything that can be exchanged for money. If people can't earn money and don't have savings they have to rely on state benefits, which is never enough. What do they do? They turn to crime, often buying and selling drugs.'

Fish: 'Drug dealing is a respectable career in many circles.'

Lee: 'That's it in a nutshell. Some states in Canada are experimenting with a basic handout to everyone over the age of eighteen – a minimum wage. It works to a degree, cuts down crime, on one side and feeds it on the other. There is still drug dealing but less robberies and fraud.'

Fish: 'Yeah, I read about that, it's called Universal Basic Income.'

Lee: 'Thanks Fish; if you analyse the motives behind Universal Basic Income it's quite laughable. The argument works well but conceals a desperate attempt to preserve the economy. Above everything else the economy has to be saved. And it's not just UBI; you saw what happened in the crash of 2008 when the banking system was under threat "save the banks, bail out the banks", sod the people. UBI is a comforter, a pacifier, and who in their right mind is going ague against it? It keeps the economy alive for a decade or two – a living breathing economy which keeps the robots in the factory busy churning out the aforementioned shit – plastic shit …'

Fish: 'More offensive than shit-shit …'

Lee: 'But propping up the banks and Universal Basic Income is only delaying the death of money and traditional economics.'

Lordy: 'So it's an environmental issue, as much as anything?'

'Enormously so, I'm worth several million,' said Lee, 'that's not a boast, it's just a boring fact, but what's the point of having all that money if there is no planet? I know the rich, I work and socialise with them. A revolution is inevitable, they know that. And whether it's a bloody revolution, with their palatial homes being ransacked or a peaceful revolution is something they can influence.'

'So it's your mates who are behind the revolution,' said Lordy.

Lee: 'Not really – some of them yes, but by no means all. Most are against it. A revolution will shatter their lifestyle and their status. What will happen to their helicopters and yachts? The idea of a moneyless society is not new, but now in 2022, the well-being of the planet makes it imperative. Britain is the country where it can happen – and it will happen.'

Fish: 'So who started it?'

Lee: 'Nobody really knows where it started. Some liken its beginnings to a tsunami – deep rumblings of tectonic plates – and Mother Earth chastising her wayward offspring. But it's not thought to be a single person or group. The idea has been around for years – it was bound to happen, and it doesn't matter where it kicks off or who started it. The important thing is that there is no violence, no looting or destruction of property. The end goal is that the people of Britain take control and become responsible for running the country; the *people* – not a biased media, a few wealthy individuals and a clueless government. But first capitalism has to draw to a close, and to achieve that you must first remove money.'

'Sounds good to me,' said Lordy. 'But what about this new bank – is it really necessary?'

'We hope not,' Lee glanced at his phone. 'Thirty-three million, the number needs to be at least fifty million before the

15

establishment sees the movement as a threat. If the new bank gets up and running, every supporter of the new government will own an equal share in it. It's put together in a similar way to the old mutual life assurance companies.'

'So I'll own my own bank,' smiled Stick.

Lee: 'When you signed up, with your name, date of birth, NI number and postcode, you signed up to the ownership of Britain. You will jointly own, and have responsibility for the running of the country.'

Stick: 'I didn't sign up for that!'

Aristotle: 'You did, Lordy signed you up last week.'

Fish: 'He can't see the screen.'

'You can withdraw at any time,' said Lee.

Stick: 'No, it's all right; I quite like the idea of owning a bank and running the country, even if it's together with these daft old sods.'

Fish: 'What about the legal implications? Last week we went shoplifting at Tesco – no arrests – no prosecutions. Mr Tesco PLC ain't gonna put up with that forever.'

Lee: 'It's complex, and difficult to keep up with, everything that happens is generated by the stakeholders – you and me. The police are inundated with crime reports beyond their capacity, they can't cope – it's another symptom of the current style of government. Under the proposals taking shape on the app the new system will have no ruling body – no government of the old type, the ruling body will be a mix of everyone and their ideas.'

Stick: 'There should be a ruling body, otherwise there will be too many ideas it'll be chaos.'

'Then suggest it,' said Lee.

Stick: 'What! How?'

Lee: 'Open up the app and under "comments" write exactly what you just said, that there should be a ruling body.'

Stick: 'Hang on, there's a trick, the way you said that …'

Lee: 'No, there ain't no trick. But because I go into the site more often than you, I'm more aware of what's going on.'

Baldy: 'What's going on then?'

Lee: 'Look, there's nothing new in this world, right. If you think there should be a ruling body, then so do hundreds or thousands of others – or none – I don't know. And this is a key point for you guys, it's exactly here and now that your mentality has to change – and develop.'

Baldy: 'How do you mean?'

Lee: 'Governments lead – the people follow. But everything is about to change – tomorrow *you* will be the government. *The people* will be the government. Our mutual responsibility is not only to ask questions but to find solutions. So, how do we elect a "ruling body" without relinquishing power to an elite ruling class of the type we are trying to break away from?'

'I still think all this stinks of communism,' said Fish.

'There is a place for leadership,' said Lee, 'a ruling body as you like to call it. But it's when that ruling body mutates and becomes manipulative and controlling – dictatorial and self-serving, well, that's when it goes wrong. Why does it go wrong? How can we prevent it from becoming corrupt?'

Fish: 'Hang on. Who are you asking?

Lee: 'You, the government.'

Stick: 'Blimey!'

Lee: 'Yeah – and that's the future. That is how it's going to be, no more passing the buck and moaning about the government – because you will be the government – together with everyone else. I'll put the suggestion on the app …'

'When's Tottenham at 'ome again?' asked Stick while Lee tapped away at his phone.

The former trader remained glued to his mobile, 'Hang on,' he said and left for the saloon bar. Together again with his associates from the city – who were also glued in silence to their gadgets – he digested the significance of the latest bulletins. Top Treasury executives had signed up to the site. Many backbenchers had also joined, and not just from the Green Party and Labour. Dyed-in-the-wool Tories were ready to follow the same path.

Fish: 'So what will happen to all those Tottenham players when they know there ain't gonna be a big fat pay cheque at the end of the month? They'll be well pissed off.'

Stick: 'Well they won't be moving to Chelsea – it'll be the USA perhaps, or Europe.'

Fish: 'Good riddance, a load of spoilt brats. Football should be for the sport, not money. The young kids of Tottenham should play for Tottenham and the same for Charlton and Liverpool.'

'I'll dig out my boots and give 'em a bit of dubbin,' said Stick.

*

'There's loads of reaction to your idea about a governing body.' Lee thrust his mobile at Stick to read.

'He can't see the screen, blind old git, give it to me and I'll read it out,' said Fish. He read with his good eye.

'The closest to a governing body can be found in *A World without Money or Politicians* published in 2017. It suggests an ever-changing selection of citizens who vote. It's a referendum-style voting system – each piece of proposed legislation or policy is voted on. The age groups are – all 12-year-olds, all 16-year-olds, those who are 20–21, 30–31, 40–41 and everyone over 50. This ensures that the responsibility for decision making is ever changing. There are healthy power breaks in order to block megalomaniacs. It's thought that voters will be on light duties so that they can focus fully on the matters in hand.

'Everyone can submit changes to, or new policy, and anyone can debate these items and are encouraged to do so. But it's only people in those age groups who vote.'

Stick: 'What! Kids voting? What do they know? Let kids be kids and leave government to grown-ups.'

Lordy: 'No, I like the idea, kids are bright and don't have all the baggage that old gits like us carry around.'

They were joined by a smartly dressed man in his early fifties, he sought out Lee. 'Oh, hi Lee, they said I'd find you here. Sorry to interrupt, gents, but I'm a bit concerned about this revolution, a left-wing uprising and the abolition of money. I signed up on the app but don't quite get it. Is it a joke? It can't be for real.'

Lee introduced him to the group, 'He works at the Treasury, so be nice to him and he might get you some free gold bars. I'll get the beers in.'

When Lee returned, Stick was consoling the Treasury official with all the authority of a founding member of the rebellion, '... so as you can see, you have nothing to worry about ...'

'I have everything to worry about. I work at the Treasury – which is all about money – if they ban money I'm out of a job, together with twelve hundred colleagues. How do I pay my mortgage? I'll be on the dole. How do I pay my bills? It's an illegal military coup, that's what it is!'

'Calm down,' said Stick, 'drink your beer and listen. If there ain't no money, there ain't gonna be no bills. Nor is there any dole. Money will be gone, *aller tout de suite*. You are right when you say it's a coup, but not a military coup. It's a justified uprising of the people. And you are one of the people – so rise up, cheers!'

'But my job, all that research and study will be wasted. That beautiful Treasury building on Whitehall will stand empty – all those records.'

Lordy: 'Okay, Treasure,' (nicknames stick in this circle of friends, which was unfortunate for the newly baptised Treasure). 'Let's put the new system to the test. What are your options? Imagine you and your Treasury mates have been given the elbow... give 'im time to think now. To hold a top job you must be pretty bright, although you disguise it well. What are your hobbies? Do you have a hobby? What would you have done had you not gone into the civil service? What is your secret yearning? And don't say lion-taming ...'

'Or accountancy ...'

'Whose round is it?'

'Ask the app ...'

Fish returned with the drinks.

'What about all them boat people,' said Baldy. 'Young blokes from all over the place, Albania for instance, there ain't no war in Albania! Slavery and the Albanian mafia they reckon. I've seen it on the news. We ain't got room for all them new people, especially young men, it's nothing but trouble.'

'Don't worry,' said Stick, 'haven't you seen the latest? Dozens of rubber dinghies heading towards Calais – full of Tory MPs.'

'Consider this,' said Lee. 'What does the Albanian mafia target – what does any criminal gang target?' He answered his own question. 'Money; in a minute there won't be any money in Britain. And there's no point in stealing because everything will be free!'

'I'm still finding it difficult picturing life without money,' said Baldy. 'Why should people work? They ain't getting paid, I don't understand it.'

Fish thought Baldy's comment a bit rich considering he'd never done a day's work in his life, but he said nothing.

'According to research,' said Lee, 'and the figures ain't totally wide of the mark, about a third of all jobs involve working directly and exclusively with money. Think of accountants, tax collectors, advertising, insurance and the majority of law – it is all about money. Now, a third of all workers will be available to do other jobs – that's a lot of people. So, the working week will be much shorter.'

Fish: 'I like the concept but it's all theoretical, I don't see it happening. Like Baldy says – why will people work? People are naturally lazy. These revolutions are okay in the short term but it always goes wrong. Look at Hitler – he gets all the people behind him – *the Jews are the problem; get rid of the Jews and everything will be fine*. But of course it ain't fine. Now we're saying *get rid of money – get rid of politicians and everything will be fine* but it won't be fine, something else will come along and there'll be a new set of problems – see what I mean?'

Lee: 'Are you suggesting that everything is fine? Because you must admit, it ain't fine, and it ain't been fine for decades.'

Aristotle: '*Ain't fine* is a bit of an understatement: Brexit, Putin's war, the fuel crisis, inflation – and Liz Truss is prime minister; and you say "it ain't fine". It's an absolute disaster! And the decline hasn't bottomed out yet, Britain is in free fall with Liz Truss's droopy drawers as a parachute.'

Baldy: 'Ha ha, a pretty picture that paints.'

Aristotle: 'And remember – things are *mighty fine* for the richest 2 per cent of the population and *pretty good* for the middle classes. The current money-based economy is divisive and not fit for purpose, nor has it been for the past fifty years. There needs to be change. Sudden and immediate change, from one day to the next – all change – no money – no politicians.'

Fish: 'Yeah, precisely, anarchy.'

Treasure: 'I'm sure it will be well organised ...'

Fish: 'And who's gonna organise it when there's no proper leadership? There'll be looting, fighting in the streets; it'll be total chaos.'

Aristotle: 'It will be up to the new government to ensure that that doesn't happen. What will the new government do, Fish?'

Fish: 'Why ask me? Oh, okay, okay, yes, I get it ... I am the new government. *Your mentality has to change, Fish – you are the new government.* I understand what you're sayin'. But I'm not geared up for that sort of thing, most ordinary people aren't. I'm too old for such radical changes.'

Aristotle: 'And that's okay, and that's how it will work, we are all different. What one person finds difficult, others find easy or at least easier. Matters will be debated, experts will be consulted, ideas will be proffered and solutions will emerge. Those who don't want to engage or feel unable to engage don't have to.'

Fish: 'So you say.'

Aristotle: 'And to pick you up on what you said about Hitler's war. Revolution and war are two very different things. Revolutions are a part of the evolution of mankind; take the Industrial Revolution – it evolved gradually, it was a peaceful change, driven by advances in technology. It was peaceful and yes there were winners and losers, life is a tough old business, we know that. But this revolution will be well thought through …'

Fish: 'Will it? There's no evidence of that – not enough to convince me. Imagine the chaos at the supermarket on the first day of the revolution. The shelves will be empty within an hour of opening. Don't think criminals won't be on the lookout for new avenues of skulduggery … like exporting whisky and building a nest egg of euros.'

Lee: 'There's a debate on the app about retaining bank cards, and changing their name to *shopping cards*. So that you do the shopping as usual; at the checkout you present your card and the purchase is registered against your name. So, you won't be able to buy five bottles of scotch at ten supermarkets – ship them off to France and collect the euros.'

Baldy: 'But I thought they'd do away with checkouts – and money – and banks; I don't get it. Now I'm confused.'

Lee: 'It prevents hoarding and over-consumption. The technical side of it hasn't been sorted yet. But as long as there's a barcode on the tin of beans it should work – and there's no bank at the other end. It's a clever idea, it means a bit more work for the IT guys but providing the prices are kept up to date, foreign visitors will be able to use their bank cards as normal, the revenue going to boost the national economy.'

(The dual problem of Brits travelling abroad and visitors holidaying in the UK had been resolved and only awaited the approval of the people. Bank cards – called shopping cards – would be used as before, cash – notes and coins – would be obsolete. Brits holidaying overseas would agree a ceiling amount before travelling, and visitors to Britain would use their bank cards in the usual way.)

Lordy: 'So does that mean there will be checks on what we spend?'

Aristotle: 'It depends on what is proposed and how the votes go – and I recognise the Orwellian echoes, but there's no Big Brother, only all our brothers and sisters around the country. We mustn't be drawn into a vacuum of naivety – there will be greed, waste and stupidity after the revolution as there is now.'

Fish: 'So that should solve the problem in Northern Ireland, too.'

Aristotle: 'To a degree, they'll get their mates to "buy" stuff for them. People will always find ways to cheat the system … but the checks mentioned earlier will prevent excesses.'

Baldy: 'Where there's the reek of money you will find liberty takers.'

Aristotle: 'Wow Baldy, and that's when you're confused.' Baldy blushed, 'It's early days,' continued Aristotle. 'The system is sound, each area – agriculture, transport, education will be analysed by experts within those fields – and among those experts there's bound to be whistle-blowers. The truth will emerge because there is freedom of speech; there is no fear of being fired, no budgets and no party politics. How many are on the app, Lee?'

Lee: 'Thirty-seven million, give or take.'

Fish: 'It all sounds very clever but I still ain't happy. I'll vote for it because I'm old and I've got nothing to lose. But there has to be motivation for people to get out of bed in the morning. And I don't see your average bloke being motivated by the promise of a bright new dawn!'

Aristotle: 'There are many motives; not least the threat to the planet. If mankind doesn't radically alter its lifestyle, there won't be a planet to live on.'

Lordy: 'And it's not exclusively *our* planet.'

Fish: 'Half the people don't care and the other half doesn't believe all that bollocks about global warming.'

Aristotle: 'We'll get the planet we deserve. And Lordy is right, we are such an arrogant species; obsessed with waistlines, eyelashes, Botox, fast cars, the latest phone and – stupid – stupid – pointless possessions. We must step aside for the plants, birds and animals or we'll lose everything!'

Baldy: 'And the viruses – and the bacteria – God didn't only create butterflies and daffodils …'

Aristotle: 'Thanks for that, Baldy. I love your bubble-bursting interjections,' – he didn't. 'Yes the viruses and bacteria, too. It must be my round.' Aristotle had been hit broadside and he knew there was no point continuing in the headwind of laughter.

*

A couple of days later, 10 September 2022

Baldy: 'It seems weird being without a queen. I've only known the Queen; it'll take time getting used to a king.'

Lordy: 'Charlie is all right, I quite like his quirky ways, tree-hugging and talking to plants.'

Fish: 'Now we've got to go through this state funeral and mock mourning. It's all pretence. No one really gives a damn. She's an old lady and she's dead. That's that.'

Baldy: 'Oh come on Fish, she's been our Queen for over seventy years. She's done a fantastic job for all that time – all that war work, and all the problems she's had with her kids – Diana and all that.'

Fish: 'Family problems, who doesn't have family problems? My sister burst into tears when she heard the Queen was dead, what's it got to do with her?' People are too sentimental. The sooner we get this revolution done and dusted, the better.'

Lordy: 'You've changed your tune. You were dead against it the other day.'

Fish: 'I'm not against it, I'm curious to see how it will unfold. I'm just concerned that it will be "out of the frying pan and into the fire". I said I'd be voting for it.'

Baldy: 'Where will drug addicts get their drugs from?'

Stick: 'I suppose drugs will become legal. Pop into the chemist's for some Fisherman's Friends, a packet of three and a couple of lines of coke!'

Lordy: 'That'll break the pushers' hearts – they'll have to queue up at the job centre together with the estate agents and tax inspectors.'

Baldy: 'Like I said the other day, you can't force people to work.'

Aristotle: 'You can't, I agree. But it'll gradually become a cultural thing; there will be peer pressure. There are families in the poorer areas of the UK where generations have never worked. There will be more focus on the individual. I guess education courses will be available – mum and dad going back to school.'

Lee: 'And there won't be poor areas because there won't be any money.'

Fish: 'That's another one of your sweeping statements, Lee. What will change? Will all those poor people wake up, and there's a Rolls-Royce sitting outside the house?'

Lee: 'Of course there won't be no fuckin' Rolls-Royce sat outside, don't be so fuckin' stupid. But there won't be any bills, no rent or mortgage. There will be groceries at the supermarket, the bus will come and the teachers will turn up to teach the kids.'

Fish: 'All right, keep your 'air on. You sound very sure. I ain't so sure.'

Lee: 'And there *will* be types who will stay in bed in the morning – they won't get up to drive the bus or whatever. There will be givers and takers, the same as now.'

Aristotle: 'As Lee said – no bills or rent – it might take days or weeks for the reality to sink in. And it will be a different experience depending on the individual's previous source of income.'

Baldy: 'How do you mean?'

Aristotle: 'Say you've got a kid who's been supplementing his family's income by working county lines; that will stop – overnight, the whole supply chain of drugs will end. That entire industry in this country will collapse. The repercussions will be felt right along the chain and as far away as Mexico. Mum works at the launderette and dad's on benefits. Mum carries on working – dad's out on a limb – what will he do? Lee, Baldy, come on, what are his options? This family man is now a parliamentarian; his role has changed, his status has changed he stands equal with every man, woman and child in Britain. What is his next step?'

Baldy: 'Wow, I never thought of it like that.'

Aristotle: 'No. And neither will he have done. How long will it take before he appreciates his new role? How long will it take for his self-image to adjust?'

Lee: 'And his self-esteem. I never thought of like that either, Aristotle you are fuckin' brilliant.'

Aristotle: 'It's the revolution that's brilliant or will be brilliant if it happens. Those types of changes in a man's self-perception translate into his chemistry – endorphins – adrenaline and dopamine begin to pump. Happiness comes from within, not from a bottle or a line of white powder. The man has the opportunity to be himself, to be fulfilled, be it through education or work.'

Fish: 'Well, bring it on then; sounds like magic, my round, same again?'

*

Lee: 'I don't understand that bloke,' he nodded towards Fish at the bar. 'I shouldn't have sworn at him like that, but he's fuckin' irritating.'

Baldy: 'No one understands Fish, not even Fish.'

Aristotle: 'He's had his troubles in the past, one particular tragedy that would have killed most people – so we cut him a bit of slack. And he's used to being sworn at so don't beat yourself up.'

Baldy helped Fish carry the beers back. 'I was thinking; what about department stores, and shops, and the high street? All that will change.'

Lordy: 'Now take it easy Baldy, all that thinking ain't good for you. High streets have been in decline for years. Half the shops are closed.'

Lee chipped in, 'Workshops – I reckon small repair workshops will spring up all over the place. David Attenborough said the biggest crime against the planet is waste. Instead of dumping the washing machine – fix it.'

Fish: 'Modern stuff can't be repaired, there are "fails" built into every design. Two-year guarantee – and twenty-five months' failure – the manufacturers don't shout that from the rooftops.'

Aristotle: 'It's called *planned obsolescence*; no sensible manufacturer is going to create an everlasting electric kettle, or even one that you can strip down and change the element. It's all about repeat sales, chuck it out and buy a new one – ching – fuck the planet. And CEOs serve their shareholders, not David Attenborough.'

Lee: 'That's bound to change; "Made in Britain" will mean that it can be repaired and that spare parts are available, it'll be good for export.'

*

25 October 2022, Britain has yet another prime minister – Rishi Sunak.

*

Baldy: 'Do you think it might spread, you know a moneyless society, the revolution – will it spread to other countries?'

Lee: 'There will certainly be focus on the UK, it's not only about economics and politics; it's about humanity and the planet.'

Baldy: 'Won't it be boring? Just imagine there won't be adverts – correct me if I'm wrong – and what about all them commercial television channels?'

Stick: 'You won't 'ave time to sit watching telly all day Baldy, you'll be basket-weaving and taking long country walks with Daphne.'

Baldy: 'It's your round Stick; the beer ain't free, not yet anyway.'

Fish: 'You need to be more imaginative Baldy. Start up your own broadcasting company – BBC.'

Baldy: 'It couldn't be worse than the BBC, political correctness to the point of being insulting to blacks. They churn out nothing but propaganda and social engineering all day long. On *Breakfast* there's two presenters talking as if the viewer has

27

the concentration span of an infant slug. *He* starts a sentence – and *she* finishes it, I've stopped watching.'

Lordy: 'What about all the strikes – ambulance, nurses, rail, postal strikes – merry Christmas to you, too. What do you think, Lee?'

Lee: 'It's the cyclic conundrum, inflation – triggered this time by Putin's war and the resultant rise in fuel prices – but the cause is irrelevant; how do governments deal with inflation?'

Lordy: 'They put up interest rates – I never understand how that helps.'

Lee: 'It doesn't help. It restricts business borrowing, so it does have some effect. But those individuals with cash deposits – the rich – receive more interest which is inflationary. It also encourages hoarding; those who can least afford it, buy certain items before prices rocket – which is also inflationary. The poor, who are in debt, pay more interest – so high interest rates work to a degree – the poor taking the hit once again. High interest rates slow inflation marginally, but as prices continue to rise the unions demand pay increases to keep pace with inflation – which is inflationary.'

Treasure: 'A mallet to crack an avocado.'

Lordy: 'What about growth? Higher interest rates slow down borrowing, which discourages business investment. Everyone is going on about growth and then the chancellor whacks up interest rates which slows growth.'

Baldy: 'So what's the answer?'

Lee: 'There ain't one. Well there is – establish an economy without money.' He tapped his index finger firmly on the beer-soaked coaster. 'A Tory chancellor doesn't give a toss about the ordinary bloke in the street. All he sees are numbers – worry, stress, suicides and self-harming don't have a column on his spreadsheet. Fuck the people, they'll survive – a few will wilt and die – but that don't matter, they breed like rabbits.' His fingers curled into his palm to form a fist. 'As long as the precious banks are safe – save the banks and fuck the people!'

Lordy: 'All right, Lee, calm down matey. Blimey …'

Baldy: 'What about the National Health Service? Even under the new regime, hospitals are still going to be under pressure, folk are still going to fall sick. And what if all the doctors clear off to America for the money?'

'Perhaps they won't get so ill so often,' said Lee inhaling deeply. 'Stress is a massive cause of illness and people will be less stressed – no money – no money worries.'

Lordy: 'The transition ain't gonna be worry free. People might wonder if there'll be enough food, or if the light will come on when they flick the switch. There will be lots of uncertainty in the early days.'

Fish: 'Yeah and if all the doctors bugger off to the US, like Baldy said …'

Aristotle: 'Ah, the beer is flowing, the debate turns on its head and doubt creeps in. O ye of little faith. You will be the government. The doctor won't just be a doctor; he or she will be a parliamentarian – as will be the electrician and the power worker. And you're right Lee, stress is a killer, but life is stressful, there isn't life without stress. The changes proposed under the revolution don't promise Utopia. Any kind of change makes us uncomfortable, people don't like change, and many won't embrace the responsibility that comes with running the country.'

Lordy: 'Yeah, I suppose you're right Aristotle, but sometimes I wonder whether I'm living in the real world. No money, no Westminster – Jack and Jill running the country … instead of up the hill.'

Aristotle: 'The early months and years will be difficult. Yes, life will be fairer and less stressful for most, but some will be worse off. There will be festering pockets of resentment and bitterness. Temptation, desire and weakness won't disappear. Greed – stupidity – vanity will still stalk the streets. As will sociopaths, bullies and psychopaths, but if the revolution becomes a reality, at least their path to power will be impeded – and that is critical. Influence won't be for sale. Every matter, every change in the law will have to pass the test of rigorous argument and debate.'

Treasure: 'All of you seem totally convinced that the revolution will be voted in. You're talking as if it's a foregone conclusion.'

Aristotle: 'You seem surprised.'

Treasure: 'Surprised? I'm *shocked*. If you're right, life as I know it is coming to an end. I'll have to build a new life, a completely new life.'

Baldy: 'It's the same for everyone and you can argue against it. And if you're in the right age bracket you can vote against it.'

Treasure: 'No, I won't vote against it – I'm fifty-one and I'll vote for the revolution. But Aristotle is right in saying the early days will be tricky.'

Aristotle: 'It will take generations. Perhaps only when our twelve-year-olds are in their fifties and running their country has become routine will they truly realise the wisdom of the revolution.'

Treasure: 'Or the folly.'

*

Britain's three prime ministers and four chancellors in 2022 were only the tip of the iceberg. Debates similar to those witnessed in the Albert were replicated in homes and workplaces throughout the land. Christmas and New Year celebrations came and went. The app had over fifty-eight million people registered – would 2023 be revolutionary?

The Inaugural People's
Parliament,
4 January 2023

The People's Government in waiting called for a pilot run of two hundred and seventy-one UK-wide parliaments. These events, would be held 'live, in the flesh' at public venues throughout the land.

If the revolution succeeded, then the parliamentary process would be a mix of the above, online debate and citizens' assemblies – the people of Britain had warmed to the app.

Westminster and the divulged parliaments of Scotland, Wales and Northern Ireland would exist in name only. Counties would attend to local matters.

The new system would be capable of calling a parliamentary session at the drop of a hat.

If ratified, a second parliament, consisting of a different group of participants would be held in two weeks' time, i.e. on 18 January 2023. A full vote by all those qualifying by age would then decide Britain's governing structure.

The nearest parliament to the Albert was the town hall and the pub volunteered a dozen or so customers, including the old boys, Treasure, Lee and Lordy. From the hundred participants, only those fitting the prescribed demographic spread would be responsible for voting; all 12-year-olds and 16-year-olds, those aged 20–21, 30–31, 40–41 and everyone over 50.

A woman in her early thirties was elected Chair. She scanned the mix of participants and began reading from the big screen. 'There are two main proposals to be debated today: that direct democracy is to replace representative democracy. And that the citizens of the United Kingdom should together form a new government and establish a new way of governing.

'That the economy should consist of two clearly defined sectors; *Domestic* – a moneyless economy to replace the current fiat economy. All goods and services will be free in the UK. *Foreign Trade* – here the pound sterling is retained and backed by the country's gold reserves, i.e. a return to the gold standard.

'There are also certain legal points to be aired in relation to the assimilation of property into public ownership.

'With deference to convention, and in the eventuality of a new government being formed, it is traditional that the reigning monarch is informed. This duty is normally performed by the new prime minister – but there won't be a prime minister, so we need to select a person or group of people to carry out this duty.

'Because these two hundred and seventy-one parliaments are a living example of direct democracy, there is an assumption that those participating today, even the sceptics, are sympathetic to the concept of direct democracy. Referenda have occasionally been used to allow the people's voice to be heard; depending on the outcome today and in a fortnight, all future policy and law will be decided within this framework.

'Debating will continue on the app for the next two weeks and on 18 January a second series of "live" parliaments, similar to today's will be repeated across the land. A critical element to the second parliament will be to set a date for the people's government to take over from the current Conservative regime. This date will be known as "Day Zero".'

'Blimey,' whispered Baldy, 'I don't know what she's talking about. Ask her what a fiat currency is. I thought a Fiat was a car.'

Stick waggled his walking stick in the air.

'Yes?'

'What's a fiat currency?'

'I have no idea; I'm reading this for the first time. Anyone know what a fiat currency is?'

Treasure: 'It's a currency not backed by any real commodity, such as gold or silver. The US dollar, the pound and the euro are all fiat – there aren't any non-fiat currencies left. It's based on trust – the people trusting the government, the currency and each other.'

Parliamentarian: 'But it says clearly on this ten-pound note,' the woman held the note and read, *'I promise to pay the bearer on demand.'*

Treasure: 'It means nothing; your tenner is nothing more than a promissory note. It saved your ancestors' carting a load of heavy metal around. Demand gold at your high street bank and they'll exchange your tenner for two fivers – or call security.'

'Okay,' said the Chair, 'thanks for that, let's debate the items in the order they are listed. The first is direct democracy.'

Parliamentarian: 'It doesn't bode well for the new government if none of us know anything about economics. How can we be expected to run the country on that basis?'

Another parliamentarian: 'But as a group we know enough. The gentleman over there knew all about the fiat currency. And, as far as I understand it, conventional trade, where money is exchanged will be exclusively with foreign countries. All goods and services within these borders will be free.'

Parliamentarian: 'Free because there's nothing on the shelves.'

Parliamentarian: 'So, in the future, the economy will have nothing to do with money. Is that so?'

Parliamentarian: 'It's difficult to understand, but exciting. I reckon the economy will be identifying resources and directing them to where they are needed, matching supply and demand.'

Treasure: 'That is, in essence, a perfectly acceptable – if a little loose – definition of the economy. And yes, the economy will have nothing to do with money.'

Parliamentarian: 'I don't understand that?'

Aristotle: 'Promises of funds for this or that project are vote catchers "we pledge the NHS (so many) millions of pounds for more doctors" despite there being no new doctors available. A veil has been neatly drawn to conceal the real problem; it clears the path for career politicians to focus on their prime aim – winning the next election.

'When the UK goes moneyless, a complete audit of the NHS will expose current imbalances – patients – ward capacity – procedures – and so on. A study of demographics will forecast the future demand for midwives – paediatricians – geriatric specialists, etc. Treatment centres for hip-replacements and cataract operations can then be put in place for the expected number of elderly patients. Citizens' assemblies provide the ideal environment for complex subjects like the NHS. The key isn't only finding and training new doctors and nurses – it's about the professors who will educate them – about the colleges – about selecting children who have the qualities and desire to go into medicine … and lengthy debates of this nature are definitely not vote catchers. And it's the same for all aspects of life, not just the NHS – defence, agriculture, education and so on.' Aristotle paused and hoped he wasn't sounding too much like a career politician. He continued: 'The revolution won't make the problems go away. But problems are easier to focus on without a fog of budgets and politics. No longer will you hear the excuse, "there is no magic money tree". The shortfall will invariably be manpower – and that is where the solutions will be found.'

Parliamentarian: 'But the manpower resources won't have changed.'

Aristotle: 'They will have changed significantly. There will be a much larger pool of labour.'

Parliamentarian: 'How can you assume that?'

Aristotle: 'Because of the empty jobs associated with money. The old economic model will be gone; no bankers, no insurance companies, no tax men, no accountants, no sales executives. These people will be retrained and redeployed – in hospitals, for example.'

Parliamentarian: 'So accountants conducting liver transplants?'

Aristotle: 'Obviously not immediately – it will take years of training, but where there's intelligence and dexterity, and a willingness to learn, why not? A bright young thirty-year-old insurance broker could easily retrain and enjoy a twenty-year career as an orthopaedic surgeon. This new parliamentary model, this type of debate, uninhibited by political point scoring or tight budgets will redistribute manpower to where it's needed. These are the debates that need to happen. A concrete five- or seven-year retraining programme is preferable to the four-year parliamentary cycle currently on offer.'

Chair: 'We first have to agree that direct democracy is what we want. You can already see the benefits, we have economic experts amongst us – we most likely have plumbers, electricians and architects. Across the whole of the UK, we have all the professions, industries, arts and crafts covered. Under the new regime they will be contributing to the whole of society rather than working to build a pension fund with fiat money.'

Parliamentarian: 'Can I just get this clear in my head?' It was an elderly gentleman. 'Parliament will be gone, political parties will be gone, politicians, the left wing, the right wing and general elections will all be gone. And in their place will be parliamentary debates like this. Is that what is proposed?'

Chair: 'Yes, pretty much so, although political parties won't be banned, at least I shouldn't think so. It depends on what parliament decides. I don't think it's a good idea to ban anything – it's better to create an environment whereby such bodies wither and die. But parliament decides. It is thought that a pattern of routine parliaments will evolve, perhaps once a week, with most of the activity being online. There is nothing to stop groups of people coming together independently to discuss any tricky matters that might pop up. I would guess that a lot of the initial activity will be restructuring the constitution and it wouldn't surprise me if it were a written constitution. But that's just my opinion. There's freedom of speech even for chairmen or chairwomen.'

Parliamentarian: 'What about the freedom to offend?'

Chair: 'I see where you're coming from, submit the question to the app, be ready with your argument and see what happens.'

Parliamentarian, the same elderly gentleman: 'I say we should go full steam ahead. It puts the people in charge and if we make mistakes, well, there's nothing new there.'

Parliamentarian: 'I disagree in the strongest terms. It's outrageous that we should be asked to decide on such important points of law. I'm not qualified, most of us aren't qualified and you're asking kids to decide. This is total madness; I can't believe this is happening.'

Chair: 'Then vote against the revolution, that is your prerogative. It's proposed that this is the way the country is to be governed in the future. If you don't want that, then vote against it. The people have lost faith in career politicians so the people have to decide. Remember, there are two hundred and seventy-one separate parliaments discussing the same remit. Just as we uncovered some financial experts, so there will be some legal experts amongst us. No one person will be making decisions on their own.'

Parliamentarian: 'It's ridiculous to think this will be voted in. British society is structured on class. The middle and upper class won't have their money stolen from under their noses. And hopefully there are enough working-class people who have strong enough aspirations to vote against it.'

Lee: 'I'm working class. I'm stinking rich and I'll be voting to go over to moneyless. I made my fortune by guessing correctly the prices on the markets. My work, if it can be called work, has contributed nothing to society. I know first-hand how the city works; only when seen from the inside you can appreciate how ludicrous our money-based system is.'

The same parliamentarian: 'I've never heard such a load of left-wing tripe. No sane person will vote for their houses to be taken away. And if city trading is corrupt, where are the regulators?'

Lee: 'You must have a short memory, mate. Don't you remember the crash of 2008? In the USA, they appointed failed bankers as regulators. They'd been forced to resign, they caused the crash for God's sake; they were the same individuals who packaged sub-prime mortgages – sold them on – and made a fortune betting on them failing! Most bank robbers do time while these leeches kept their money, and walked out of their bank jobs into bank regulation. You know nothing about banking or your precious money.'

The same parliamentarian: 'That's in America, this is Great Britain. It's you who know nothing! You are using false logic. How would you prevent murders, ban kitchen knives?'

Lee: 'Yes "That's in America", but geography is irrelevant, the US dollar however, is highly relevant – critical in fact. Since the 1970s, the US dollar has played the role of gold standard – that was a clever move by Nixon.'

Treasure, addressing the same man: 'You are also forgetting the Royal Bank of Scotland. Let me remind you – it was your money if you are a taxpayer, it was you who bailed them out; and Northern Rock, remember the queues? And don't forget HSBC, and the financial collapse in Iceland. That's why money has to go. We elevate psychopaths into key positions – both in banking and government. They gorge on power and money. And the irony is that they are not breaking the law – the law makers – the government, are complicit – they deregulated – their only thought is re-election – a four-year cycle. There exists a seemingly buoyant economy – the people have homes – everyone is happy. Until the bubble bursts, the banks collapse and the families are chucked out of their homes. In reality money doesn't exist. The debate or question should be "when do we admit that money doesn't exist?" This would lead to a more relevant exploration of the facts – with the appendage "when did money die?"'

Some clapped but many had lost the trail. Treasure continued: 'In 2007/8 in the US, the markets morphed into an elaborate state-approved casino. The bail-outs couldn't have happened without the country printing more money – meaning a larger national debt. Can't you see it? Money has to go.'

Another parliamentarian, a professor of economic history: 'I agree. The evidence is indisputable, look back to the US Depression of 1920/21, followed quickly by the Wall Street Crash in 1929. In the hundred years since, there has been a series of crashes and crises, Black Mondays, Black Wednesdays, recessions, dot-com bubbles and then, as has already been mentioned, the 2008 great recession. It's always the rich who get to keep the money and always the poor who take the hit. When money has been eradicated there will be no poor.'

Lordy: 'You're right, mate. And when politicians have gone, the people can get on with running the country.'

First parliamentarian: 'You're all fucking mad, I'm out of here, next stop Heathrow Airport.'

Chair: 'Order, let's just calm down; this shan't become a slanging match while I'm Chair. I think you've all made some very interesting points.'

A hand was raised and a sixteen-year-old girl stood up. 'That man's right, the one who stormed out. It's not fair. My dad owns some houses which he bought and renovated, he rents them out to people at a fair price, he has worked very hard all his life and now you are going to take his houses away from him – that is pure theft. It's not fair.'

Chair: 'Yes your father will be negatively affected when the state assumes ownership of all property. Think about your father's situation and try to work your way through to a solution. That is the purpose of these parliaments. Britain is attempting to make life fairer for everyone, but in doing so, is bound to make it less fair for some individuals.'

Aristotle: 'There will be some collateral damage and your father may be a victim of this. I'm pretty certain the other parliaments around the land are hearing similar stories. Your father is a capitalist, a hard-working honourable man, no doubt, but a capitalist nonetheless. Capitalism will end in Britain. Your father's pursuit of wealth will be curtailed and he will have to rethink his life.'

Girl: 'So what you are saying is, *tough*.'

Chair: 'Make sure you speak to me afterwards. I am merely the Chair of this meeting; I have no more power than you or your father. It's the debating and the voting that will count.

'The next point is closely related to the previous one. Money laundering in this country has long been linked to foreign criminals buying properties via nefarious cartels and investment companies based in tax havens abroad.

'Would the UK's confiscation of foreign-owned properties be in breach of international law?'

Parliamentarian: 'Confiscate the properties and let the international lawyers try to sue us!'

The Chair continued. 'It is understood from comments on the app that the protection of sterling is critical; we have to be able to trade with other nations. Our currency has to be credible and opinion suggests that this can only be achieved by fixing it to gold. Credibility is also dependant on legitimacy – here, under international law. It's important not to expose Britain to a raft of legal cases. Parliament will debate this item further when we have been advised by a team of experts.'

Parliamentarian: 'You keep mentioning experts. What experts? That sounds dodgy to me. Who is going to appoint these people? I never trust experts.' There were mumblings in agreement.

Parliamentarian: 'If we are to run the country we mustn't be afraid to upset a few international bodies. Timidity is not part of the British psyche!'

Parliamentarian: 'Nor should we go out of our way to agitate the international community. Diplomacy, I would respectfully suggest, *is* a part of the British psyche.'

Chair: 'All of this is noted. But please, we must try to be less suspicious of experts. If there are potholes in the road – there are experts at repairing them …'

Parliamentarian: 'Are there?'

Chair: 'Perhaps there aren't now, but there will be if the people of Britain want there to be. And I hope they engage tarmac experts … not ear, nose and throat specialists.

'Please remember, we are not party politicians, there will be no lies, and there will be no money in circulation and therefore no scope for creative accounting. There will be no hands in the till – there will be no till. As for the "experts" – we have to accept that the world of finance we are leaving behind us is complex. There are people from the Treasury and the legal profession who know this world. We have experts here today who have helped in our understanding of unfamiliar fields. We need to be able to call on experts often, we cannot deny the past. Their findings will always be debated by parliament and citizens' assemblies – and parliament will have the final word – now let's move on.'

'She's a bloomin' good chairwoman,' whispered Stick. 'Cheeky, too.'

Parliamentarian: 'Among the overseas property owners there must be some legitimate ones. Will they be adequately compensated?'

Treasure: 'Good point. I guess it will be up to them to prove the legitimacy of ownership including a money trail. They should be paid what is due to them from our gold-backed currency. Legal experts and the fraud squad need to oversee each case.'

*

It was drafted into the minutes that:

All land and properties owned by companies or individuals abroad would be treated exactly the same as those legitimately owned by UK residents and corporations, i.e. they would be taken into common ownership. The legal consequences will be dealt with as and when they arise, with compensation paid in those cases where evidence of legal ownership was documented and an untainted money trail was proved by the claimant.

'The final item to be debated – but not voted on until 18 January – *When should Day Zero be triggered?*

'Here is a draft copy of the "Day Zero Declaration" for your comments and suggestions.' The Chair read from the screen. 'The Day Zero Declaration hereby gives notice to: the Citizens of the United Kingdom, the incumbent Conservative government, the Labour Party, all other political parties, the devolved parliaments of Scotland, Wales and Northern Ireland:

That the Citizens of the United Kingdom – every man, woman and child – will this day (date) **form a new government.**

'I hope that is clear.'

*

Treasure: 'Why wait two weeks? Every hour of delay is an hour wasted. Words don't house the homeless. Words don't help the heart attack patient waiting in the ambulance queue. Day Zero will free-up a massive workforce ready to roll up their sleeves and turn this country into a model that will inspire the world. I envisage this new, *government of the people*, being replicated in every corner of the planet, dictators will be overthrown, communist and capitalist regimes will capitulate and the people of the world will be free to rule – let's start today – now!'

Baldy, whispering to Lordy: 'Blimey, he's changed his tune.'

Parliamentarian: 'Stirring stuff, but just hang on, there's no need to rush. How do we know there will be enough votes to proceed? Is everything ready? Are we fully prepared?'

Treasure: 'The sooner we start managing this country directly and sympathetically, the sooner we can get the homeless off the streets and repair the care …'

Chair: 'Stop, stop, stop. You digress; the date is to be decided in two weeks. Suggest a date; there are others waiting to speak.'

'Yes, I digress, I apologise – let's do it on 18 January – let that be Day Zero.'

Parliamentarian, an elderly man: 'What about the Army? Yes, 18 January seems a good proposal, but before we go any further the Army needs to be clear where it stands. The Army is loyal to the realm – which means King Charles and his government.'

Parliamentarian: 'And what about the Air Force and the Royal Navy?

Parliamentarian: 'And the police force?'

Treasure: 'I believe the reigning monarch, the King, is Commander-in-Chief of the armed forces.'

Parliamentarian: 'But it's the prime minister who decides, if we go to war for example … and there won't be a prime minister!'

Parliamentarian: 'What about the secretary of state?'

Parliamentarian: 'And the Ministry of Defence?'

Baldy: 'Yeah, you can't be too careful with Putin on the loose.'

Aristotle: 'Whoever it is now is irrelevant, come Day Zero it will be the people who decide.'

Parliamentarian: 'Agreed but it'll be the generals and admirals who decide the day-to-day running of the armed forces.'

'And the Air Chief Marshal,' said the first man who, with his handlebar moustache looked as though he might be the Air Chief Marshal. 'My point is that the leaders of the armed forces should be kept abreast of developments, it is they who defend the country. And defence is damned important right now, excuse my French.'

Chair: 'All the forces are fully aware of developments, as are the civil service and the NHS – their leaders have free access to the app. They are citizens of the United Kingdom and, as such, will have no more or less power than anyone else. It wouldn't surprise me if they were represented at today's parliaments, here and around the country.'

Stick, in a whisper: 'She's on the ball!'

Chair: 'I'm sure the other parliaments would have picked up on those points, too; very efficient. The only suggested date is 18 January 2023; I will add that to the notes.'

The worried sixteen-year-old girl: 'I would like to volunteer to meet with the King and tell him about the new government.' She blushed at the applause. The Chair asked if she had thought any more about her father's situation.

'Yes, I think he will be okay, he is very resourceful. I am sure he could teach carpentry at a school, proper woodwork and cabinetmaking, not heavy building stuff like fitting windows and doors. And he used to play the trumpet in a jazz band before he met my mum … that's how they met—'

The Chair cut her short. 'Thank you very much. I'll suggest that you should meet with the King.'

Every part of this revolutionary parliament (and the other two hundred and seventy) was recorded. The contributions would be authenticated for accuracy and summarised.

Parliamentarian: 'There are only fifty-three million over-eighteen-year-olds in the UK – I just googled it – so a lot of kids must have registered. What we don't know though, is how many of the overall number oppose the revolution. The only way to argue against revolution is from within. So, what percentage is *for*, and how many are *against*? That's what I'd like to know.'

Parliamentarian: 'We won't know until the vote in two weeks' time. But what worries me is how many of those names are false? What is the security on registrations? They could be people abroad, Russian spies or double registrations. This is parliament we are talking about; it must be secure.'

Parliamentarian: 'That's a good point, security is paramount. We can say with certainty that a majority of the citizens of the UK are on the app.'

Parliamentarian: 'Look, it has been suggested that those registered on the app will almost certainly include a significant element of dissenters and perhaps even fraudsters or foreign spies. The concept of dumping politicians and letting the people get on with running the country is fairly clear-cut. But how many will vote for a moneyless economy? How many of us really understand economics to the degree where we can confidently make such a decision? At the moment the pound is falling, everyone is buying dollars, gold and euros. We can't stop the run on the pound until we have total control. And that is why we can't dilly-dally. I guess one of the drawbacks of such a large body of people is "speed of decision-making" or lack of it more precisely.'

Parliamentarian: 'I agree,' started a middle-aged, well-dressed woman.

The Chair interrupted. 'Agree with which point? The gentleman made several. Please be precise.'

'About our lack of competence around economics and money, but I suggest that as a body we know enough. We have been told that money, the pound, the dollar, the euro – all the main currencies, are not backed by anything. There is no gold standard and nor has there been for some time. Money and debt are primarily a question of trust; and that trust has expired. From Day Zero, the pound will have the backing of our gold reserves, the only currency in the world to have such backing, which means that a falling pound is nothing to worry about, at least while the price of gold is rising. Have I understood that correctly?'

'Yeah,' said Baldy, 'spot-on darlin".

'Don't call me darling.'

'Sorry darlin', oops, sorry love … er, madam.' A sharp tap to the shin from Stick's walking stick shut him up.

Parliamentarian: 'I still have no idea about what's going on,' said a young man, aged about twenty-one or twenty-two. 'I work in a factory on an assembly line. Should I turn up for work after we go over to moneyless? I won't get paid so why should I work?'

'A very good question,' said the Chair. 'Perhaps we could ask for more contributions from the floor. Put your hand up if you would like to comment. Keep it brief, name your job and if you think that you will continue working.'

Parliamentarian: 'People won't go to work and you're mad if you think they will.' It was a young lady and she nodded in the direction of the man. 'Thanks for adding a little sanity to this debate. Can't you see that the country will grind to a standstill? People won't work. Who would be mad enough even to get out of bed when they know they won't get paid? There are enough lazy sods on the dole as it is. I am terribly worried about what's happening.'

Several hands went up.

Parliamentarian: 'I own a veterinary clinic. Of course I'll carry on working. I won't have to pay my staff, or rent and rates. No electricity bills, free transport to and from the clinic. I just hope my staff turn up for work, too.'

Parliamentarian: 'I'm a police officer and I'll carry on as normal, but what effect will a moneyless economy will have on crime? No money signals the end of drug dealers, and without drug dealers you'll see a sharp reduction in shoplifting and muggings, I don't reckon I'll be very busy if the revolution is voted in.'

Parliamentarian: 'I'm a teacher, so yes, I will carry on as normal. My mortgage will be written off – I presume, and I won't have any bills. If the car breaks down the garage will pick it up and I won't have to pay.'

Parliamentarian: 'I'm a motor mechanic, and I'll be working as normal so you're right, we'll pick up your car, and my kids go to your school so don't be late.'

Parliamentarian: 'I'm an independent financial adviser and mortgage broker so I'll be out of work. I've always had ambitions to be a professional footballer, but they will be unemployed same as me. Anyone fancy a game of footie in the park when we've finished here?'

Parliamentarian: 'I'm a gardener at the park, I reckon we could renovate the changing rooms and get the showers working now that there will be no more cutbacks. I assume all this will mean the end to cutbacks.'

Parliamentarian: 'I'm a builder; I'll contact the council and see if we can help out. I'm looking forward to this new way of life.'

Parliamentarian: 'I'm a care worker and would encourage any financial advisers or professional footballers to contact the NHS for redeployment.'

Chair: 'Okay, thanks for that. It's by no means conclusive but it does give an idea of what people are thinking. Are there any more dissenters? We need a complete picture.'

Slowly hands went up; a man in his forties spoke first. 'Can't you see that this won't work? The Army will surely put the revolution down. What is being proposed here and around the UK is tantamount to ending our traditional way of life.'

Aristotle: 'Yes, it will end some traditions, many of them bad. Class and privilege – rich and poor – left wing and right wing and political correctness for example. What is tradition and what is decay? Fifty years ago we listened to the radio, read the paper and believed everything. It's not like that now – politicians have no hiding place – they've been rumbled.

'Take a closer look at political correctness, PC is the same as pretending, and pretending is the same as lying – most often self-deceit. *Political correctness* is poorly named; it has nothing to do with politics or correctness. Originally coined nearly a hundred years ago to protect the feelings of vulnerable minorities it has morphed into a ban on straight talking. Political correctness is downright deceitful and I hope there will be no place for deceit in this new government. Think back to the way the police tip-toed round the Pakistani gangs of child molesters – political correctness. How did Jimmy Savile go undetected for all of his perverted life? Because he raised so many millions for charity! Money and political correctness – is there a more toxic mix? Good old Sir Jimmy! Why are there so many "quota" government leaders and MPs? Political correctness – votes – it's bending over backwards not to offend minorities. People dare not speak these words for fear of being called racist, and those who would call the revolution left wing, or the likes of me communist, are probably now thinking "that old boy is right wing". And that is why left wing and right wing will evaporate if this new government of the people take over the running of the UK.

'This country must embrace the changes proposed in the revolution. No more restraint; unsavoury thoughts must be spoken; unsavoury thoughts are preferable to saccharin-sweet lies. Dump left wing, right wing and dump political correctness. Sensitive matters must be aired – the clear thinking *new broom* of revolution has to sweep a clean path to the truth – please or offend.'

Parliamentarian: 'And how will the decisions be enforced? Say, for example, it's decided that capital punishment is to be reinstated. Who will be responsible for giving the lethal injection or pulling the trapdoor? This hasn't been properly thought through.'

Aristotle pointed to the speaker. 'And there, sir, you have it in a nutshell. I am so glad you spoke those words. It's all about attitude. Our thinking has to change. You speak as a citizen speaks to its government – I, sir, am not your government; I am your fellow parliamentarian. We have equal power. Under the new regime *you* are a critical part of the decision-making process – setting the agenda – debating and voting. It's an excellent point that you make – put it on the app – share it with everyone. Any decisions about law change and law enforcement will be thoroughly thrashed out in parliaments and citizens' assemblies. And people like you will vote.'

Parliamentarian: 'It's communism! Why don't you admit it's communism?'

Aristotle: 'Okay, let us say for a moment that this new system of government is communism – and communism is the word that describes it most accurately. *Communism* is a tainted word. What's happening here in the UK is the *people's* revolution, a peaceful bloodless revolution; a beautiful, inclusive revolution of honest dialogue, of robust debate and courageous compromise. We have to shelve the concept of left wing and right wing. That categorisation destroys the fidelity of the matter under discussion. Mention, for example, immigration, and a right-wing alarm sounds. Mention aid to a Third World country and a left-wing flag is raised.

'To label a thought or persuasion as left or right is to condemn it before any meaningful dialogue has even begun. Debate has to be at a different level and only when there are no financial consequences and no party politics – can that level of honesty be attained – then and only then.'

'Go Aris!' shouted Baldy. Treasure clapped and Stick whispered in his ear, 'This is all off the cuff, he's brilliant.'

Aristotle continued: 'There is no dictator, there is no oppressive regime. We are the regime. There will be a refreshing absence of lying politicians ducking and diving with their own egos, and a four-year term in office at the top of their priority list. Those of us here and the sixty-seven million men, women and children are charged with building a constitution with checks and balances to bar psychopathic megalomaniacs and prevent any one faction from becoming too powerful. There will be no secrets; everything said here will be available for scrutiny around the country and, likewise, we can monitor what is being discussed in Lancashire or Cornwall – there won't be any dirty deals or back-stabbing as there are under the old system.' Aristotle pointed towards the man who asked the question.

'If you look around the world you will find *no* communism. You will find the Chinese Communist Party – but China isn't a communist country – it's a very successful trading nation and a fully paid-up member of the capitalist fraternity, as is Russia.' Aristotle stood tall and pulled his old back straight.

'Most of the countries flying the communist flag are oppressive, tyrannical dictatorships. Let me ask you this question. If the mothers and fathers of communist Russia had a voice, would Russia have invaded Ukraine? If this UK version of *communism*, as you would like to call it was established in Russia – would there be a war now? No, because Putin is a dictator. *State-sponsored capitalism* is not communism. Russia, China and North Korea are not communist countries! There are no communist countries in existence.'

Parliamentarian: 'So, it's communism but we're not to call it communism – what do we call it – socialism – liberalism? Or should we give it a new name? Great British "Silly Sodism" for example.'

Aristotle: 'Ha ha, yes a new name, a good idea, there will be plenty of marketing experts with time on their hands, perhaps we should consult them – or have a competition – *Win a weekend away in North Korea*. I hope the winning name has reference to British fair play and common sense.' Aristotle looked again at those who had spoken. 'You are right to be apprehensive; it would be daft not to be. Vote honestly, *think* – dwell briefly on leaders of the past, from demons like Hitler to salad vegetables like Liz Truss and all those between. Thank you for your indulgence.' The retired welder sat down to a gentle ripple of considered applause.

'Very inspiring,' said the Chair, 'but let me remind you of the agenda.' She pointed to the screen. 'It is time for those who qualify to vote.'

*

That direct democracy is to replace representative democracy. And that the citizens of the United Kingdom should together form a new government and establish a new way of governing.

For – 65%   Against – 24%   Don't know – 11%

That the economy should be split into two clearly defined categories; Domestic and Foreign Trade.

Domestic – *a moneyless economy to replace the current fiat economy.* **Foreign Trade** – *here the pound sterling is retained and backed by the country's gold reserves, i.e. a return to the gold standard.*

For – 63%   Against – 27%   Don't know – 10%

'Thank you, parliament. This is an historic day and there will be a repeat in a fortnight. Keep your eyes on the app and follow the voting results from around the country. All the results are open for your perusal.'

It was established that fifty-eight million people had registered on the app – was that enough? It was an indication that the general public was fully engaged, but was revolution in the air? How many would vote *for* and how many *against*?

Fleet Street followed events but twenty-four hours behind. Newspaper content was limited to Putin's war, other foreign news, sport, opinion and, importantly, readers' letters – which were carefully filtered. Those selected for publishing had a definite dislike of the revolution. A successful revolution was not in the interests of the press moguls. But activity on the app and the two hundred and seventy-one parliaments could not be ignored; their reporting was limited to negative spin and caustic remarks.

The Sun: 'Yes, there are around fifty-eight million folk on the app, but how many are just curious? The editor and all us journalists are on the app. None of us will be voting for a revolution, we are not buying this left-wing hot air. WIN A TRIP TO TURKEY – plus spending money.'

Financial Times: 'Two hundred and seventy-one powerless parliaments held in every corner of the United Kingdom. Powerless they may be, so far, but as sterling plummets, focus is on a mortally wounded Tory government.'

The Guardian: 'The British public has lost faith in the establishment – there are echoes of Magna Carta …'

Daily Mail: 'The last referendum gave us Brexit and now the lefties want everything to be decided by referendum …'

As the right-wing press watched their power dwindle, the people wrote their own headlines on the app's metaphorical front page.

Even the more liberal publications were hedging their bets but had their concerns. What would be the point of their existence without advertising revenues? What was the point of advertising when marketing and commerce were about to become obsolete? How would they sell newspapers when there was no money? As for the dissemination of information … people were now using the app to keep up to date.

The blanket rethink that gripped the whole nation was affecting the editors of these publications. Perhaps the app itself would be their new mischief-making tool. It was easy; everyone registered on the app was a bona fide parliamentarian!

Parliamentarian: 'Politics is a specialised art; left-wing mob rule is proposing to hand over our country to – among others, children and criminals in jail. What kind of Britain can you expect with this combination of naivety and criminality? Vote no, trust the tried and tested conventional political process.

Northern Ireland

Nervous Catholics and suspicious Protestants made up the majority of the delegates at the eleven parliamentary meetings in Northern Ireland. They were joined by a smattering of people of other religions and those who abstained from any form of religion. The sentiment was one of curiosity and 'not wanting to miss out' rather than a feeling of pioneering renewal.

The political climate was indeed very different to that of the rest of the UK; the unrest, the border, the religious disharmony and unfinished business with Europe hung like a cloud. The last thing Northern Ireland needed was a revolution – or would one last revolution right the injustices of the past?

Many south of the border watched with benign curiosity – could this revolutionary system of governance work in the republic? The torment that shaped their country emanated from the British ruling class, not the British people, who, it would seem, would soon be the new ruling body.

A dozen or so people living in the Republic requested a version of the app; the British government in waiting granted their wishes without delay. The app spread quickly and within a few days, 70 per cent of the Republic of Ireland had access to the app. The structure was the same – the same hardware – the same scope for self-management – but the app was not integrated with the British one. The people of the Republic of Ireland cautiously edged forward and planned their own preliminary parliaments.

The voting results for Northern Ireland:

That direct democracy is to replace representative democracy. And that the citizens of the United Kingdom should together form a new government and establish a new way of governing.

For – 54%   Against – 42%   Don't know – 4%

That the economy should be split into two clearly defined categories; Domestic and Foreign Trade.

Domestic – *a moneyless economy to replace the current fiat economy.* **Foreign Trade** – *here the pound sterling is retained and backed by the country's gold reserves, i.e. a return to the gold standard.*

For – 61%   Against – 29%   Don't know – 10%

Checks and Balances

On the app: It is widely acknowledged how easy it is for power-hungry individuals to crawl to the top – and how quickly people forget.

Orwell alarm: An app entry proceeded by *Orwell alarm* would warn of an individual or group suspected of attempting to secure power.

Rethink: An inundation of app entries with this prefix would call for a second look at a recent change of legislation or a new dictate. The item would be revisited. Mistakes are inevitable but not to rectify them is unacceptable and this regime has systems in place to cope with that.

Stasi alarm: Law and order are important but so is freedom of the individual; getting the balance right is not always easy and app entries with this prefix will draw attention to over-zealous legislation.

Stupidity virus: No revolution can wipe out stupidity and this alert will prevent wasting time on trivial debates.

No solution: Not all problems have solutions – so admit it – shelve the matter and return to it later.

The Second Parliament,
18 January 2023, 10 a.m.

The eyes of the world were on the UK – the men, women and children of rebellious Britain were centre stage.

By demand, the number of parliaments was increased to three hundred and twenty and the amount of participants was tripled to three hundred. These randomly selected citizens gathered to be part of the historic proceedings (eleven of these were in Northern Ireland, one for each region).

All the debates were to be broadcast on separate channels; technicians volunteered and created a channel for each of the parliaments. The people of Britain were able to tune in to whichever parliament they chose. Voting would be both online and at the live parliaments.

Westminster met on the same day, perhaps with capitulation in mind, or perhaps plans of a more sinister nature were festering.

*

An early morning drinking session at the Albert was unusual, but so was today's event. The old codgers had had their moment a fortnight earlier, and now, at the town hall, new faces took their place. A man in his fifties, a headmaster from a local school, was selected to chair the debate and he opened the parliament.

*

Lordy and his wife served beer, the smell of bacon wafted through from the kitchen and screens showed the parliament from the town hall.

Vigorous debate had continued uninterrupted following the first two hundred and seventy-one parliaments. Comments, disagreements and points of law had been tossed back and forth across cyberspace 24/7 – often it was two steps forward and one back – but progress was made.

*

The Chair took his place on the stage and the parliamentarians settled and focused on the big screen.

Chair, reading from the screen: 'Voting at the inaugural parliament indicated an appetite to shift to direct democracy and to implement the changes to the economy as debated. However not the whole of the voting public has yet cast their vote. Only those attending the live parliaments voted. Today, all qualifying voters have the opportunity to vote – here, at the other three hundred and nineteen parliaments and online.'

There was no surprise at the Albert, but a round of applause and a free round of beer celebrated the moment.

'Although debate is not ruled out, please keep it to matters of procedure rather than churning over what has gone before. We have the rest of our lives to debate.

'Today's agenda: *The endorsement of the vote from the two hundred and seventy-one parliaments on 4 January 2023.*

'*The approval of a written constitution:* A draft constitution has been drawn-up and has been available for perusal on the app since 6 January 2023. Remember, this is a draft document – it is a starting point; amendments to the constitution will be ongoing – many think never-ending.

'*The date on which to trigger Day Zero:* If there is majority in favour – as outlined below; *when* do the people take over the running of the United Kingdom?

'A vote *for* (requiring a majority of 50%) will mean that the people of the UK will govern their country on the agreed basis of direct democracy via online debate, multiple live parliaments and citizens' assemblies. The economy will be moneyless within our borders. The pound will be backed by our gold reserves and used for foreign trade only. All the broader details are written into the constitution.

'A vote *against* will suspend this project for twelve months; the economy in its present form will continue and power will remain with Westminster. If, in a year, there is appetite for it, parliaments of this type will resume.

'A majority *don't know* vote will trigger another two weeks of debate, a third parliament and more voting.

'Voting today must be completed by 4 p.m. (16.00 hours).

'Checks and double-checks on the voters have taken place. Each voter is registered with their full name, address, date of birth and National Insurance number, and each has been vetted by two referees who are doctors, justices of the peace or ministers of the church.

'The qualifying voters are; all 12-year-olds, all 16-year-olds, those aged 20–21, 30–31, 40–41 and everyone over 50.'

*

'I endorse the outcome of the voting in the inaugural parliaments of 04-01-2023.

Qualifying voters can start voting now. Your options are;

For   Against   Don't know

'I have read and understood the new constitution as it stands and appreciate that ongoing upgrading will be a part of the parliamentary process.

Qualifying voters can start voting now. Your options are;

For   Against   Don't know

'That this day (enter your chosen date here) in the UK, a government consisting of every man, woman and child will assume the running of the country. Policy and law will be debated online, in live parliaments and citizens' assemblies. The voting section of the population will decide. This is direct democracy.

'Confirm your suggested date for Day Zero;   **DD-MM-20__**.

'Voting ends at 4 p.m. today, and if votes *for* carries the motion by more than 50%, the changes will come into effect at 12 noon on the chosen day.

'Parliamentary debate is now suspended until 4 p.m. when the results will be made known.'

*

Baldy: 'So, if the vote goes against, everything stops for a year. That can't be right; we're poised to kick out those lying, scheming politicians—'

Aristotle interrupted: 'Direct democracy, Baldy, the most difficult challenge with this type of democracy is accepting defeat. We each have our own idea of right and wrong. Parliamentarians of the new government – and that's all of us – have to understand that it is the vote that matters. The success or failure of the system depends on the reaction of those outvoted. Do you recall what I said a fortnight ago at the town hall? "Honest dialogue, robust debate and *courageous compromise*." It is the *courageous compromise* that has to be exercised with the most stringent discipline – individual self-discipline. And *that* is the trickiest aspect of direct democracy. You may also recall that a parliamentarian asked how the voting decisions would be enforced, and I skirted around that question – not out of cowardice and not because I didn't know the answer, but because the complexity, delicacy and critical nature of the explanation was too important to skimp within those time restraints. Accepting the vote is fundamental to true democracy. The most critical, single course of action – or inaction more to the point, is to accept the vote. Accept it like death. Swallow the bitter pill and move on.

Cases that can be reworked will be resurrected later with fresh argument, but sometimes you trudge off a muddy rugby pitch having lost. And that's that. Have a pint with the opposition and play them again next season.'

Stick: 'Yeah, good stuff Aristotle, but don't forget to vote. Look the votes for are leaping ahead.'

The votes were shown on a separate screen and already at 10.30, the votes stood at 21 million *for*, 13.5 million *against*, and 1.5 million *don't knows*. The most popular inauguration date was today, Wednesday, 18 January 2023.

*

The Chair read from the screen at the town hall and drinkers at the pub followed events.

'**The following statement only applies if the proposals are carried.** Within our borders, all goods and services are free depending on availability. The suggestion that all retail outlets should be closed to prevent panic buying (probably the wrong term) for the first twenty-four hours of freedom was rejected following an online vote.

'It will take some time to get used to the new system and restraint is called for. Remember this is your decision, only take from the supermarket the things you need. All goods will require your shopping card (your former bank card) to be swiped before you take delivery of them. You won't be able to buy ten Lamborghinis on the first day. We don't want empty shelves at the supermarkets and food rotting in the fridge at home.

'Carry on as normal. Turn up for work and school so that the chain of responsibility is maintained. If everyone does their bit, the transition will be seamless. Transport will run, the factories will produce, the farms and food manufacturers will ensure the supply of food and children will work at their lessons. *You* will be governing the country, there is no Big Brother watching.

'Bear in mind that there are still around nine million UK residents who are not registered on the app. Many of these will be babies and small children and remember that it isn't compulsory to be a member of the government; this is the individual's decision. Information is available via non-electronic means –

newspapers, public libraries and notice boards in public places in various languages. But if you see someone who needs help – help them.

'Those with occupations that will be superfluous in the new environment, please make yourself known to places of employment where you think you could be most useful. You can contact the town hall, job centre or other public offices for help. If you are in a branch that needs workers ...' the screen went blank.

The Heist

'The Internet's down,' said Lordy.

At 10.35 in the Albert, the screen went blank and the lights went out. At the live parliaments around England, Scotland and Wales, the lights went out. Mainland Britain had no electricity, only Northern Ireland remained unaffected and voting continued there.

The drinkers went out into the winter rain. 'It's the mains – everything's down. No electricity. No Internet. No mobile phone signals.'

'Sabotage!'

'It could be coincidence,' said Baldy. 'Do you reckon it's just local or the whole of London?'

'It could be the whole of the country,' said Treasure, 'this is the Tory Party in its death throws.'

Stick: 'Do you really think it's the government? What can we do? Everything happens on the app, we can't see what's happening in any of the parliaments.'

Aristotle: 'There's no need to panic, they can't stop the vote, the three hundred and twenty parliaments will vote manually and online voting will continue as soon as the power returns. Westminster can't keep the lights out forever.'

Baldy: 'Then why have they cut the power? What's the point if they know they can't stop the voting? There must be another reason.'

'You're right, Baldy,' said Aristotle. 'What are those Tory bastards up to? If it is sabotage, what long-term damage do they think they can achieve with a short-term power cut?'

Baldy: 'Perhaps they're gonna nick the gold – you know, from the Bank of England.'

Fish: 'What the fuck are you talking about, Baldy? I can't work out how your brain works. No more beer for you.'

Baldy: 'That's a point, Lordy, are the beer pumps still working?'

Lordy: 'Craft beer – powered by atmospheric pressure and the cunning use of vacuum – travels magically from seasoned oak barrels in the cool of the cellar to the brim of your pristine glasses. No need for the Internet, algorithms, digitalisation or electricity.'

'Thank God for that. Got any candles, Lordy?'

'I'll dig some out.'

Stick: 'The power is bound to be back soon. What do we do in the meantime?'

Fish: 'Drink beer and wait. I reckon the people of Britain will vote it through. I'm kinda getting used to the idea of being a parliamentarian.'

Lee: 'What's that noise? It sounds like a helicopter. Go and have a look, Baldy.'

Treasure: 'See it off, Baldy; it's disturbing the tranquillity of the moment. It sounds really low; it must be the Army trying to sort out the power.'

Aristotle: 'The power, which is about to change hands … ha ha …'

Lordy: 'You sound very confident.'

Aristotle: 'Yeah, but I'm not. Not really. This power cut can't just be the Tories throwing their toys out of the pram …'

Baldy returning: 'Did you hear that? It was flying really low. I thought it was going to land at one point. A military helicopter, American I think, it had an eagle on the side.'

Lordy: 'That's weird …'

Aristotle: 'What was that you said earlier, Baldy?'

Baldy: 'About the beer?'

Aristotle: 'No, about the Tories nicking the gold.'

Baldy: 'Ha, I was only joking. Why would they nick their own gold?'

Aristotle: 'They might not be nicking it, just moving it to the USA for safekeeping. What do you think, Treasure?'

Treasure: 'The gold can't be stolen, it's impossible; security is layered – both reinforced concrete and electronically.' He didn't let on that he was party to the security at the Bank of England. Treasure, together with four others, had a code to the vaults. It required the presence of all five to complete the code before gaining access to the gold. 'They could never smash their way in, and a series of codes have to be completed before gaining authorised access to the vaults.'

Lordy: 'Bad luck, Baldy, no James Bond raid on the Bank of England. Let us sit patiently in the gloaming and sip the golden nectar.' He found some candles and circles of yellow light punctured the gloom.

Baldy: 'What if they are planning to move the gold to the United States. Without the gold reserves we won't be able to trade with the rest of the world. The revolution will collapse and the Tories will continue to govern. There is probably an American aircraft carrier in the Thames right now waiting to cart off our gold reserves. What do we do?'

Fish: 'Forget it, Baldy, our gold is safe. Shut up, relax and drink your beer.'

Treasure: 'The revolution can still succeed. It doesn't matter where the gold reserves are. They belong to the realm and are British property. During the Second World War, they were secretly moved to Canada, the location is irrelevant, it's Britain's gold.'

Lordy: 'Then why the helicopter? Why the power cut? The timing, too – the day of the vote, it all seems dodgy to me. And all the cloak and dagger; this ain't 1943, these are different times. What if the Yanks are after the gold?'

Baldy: 'Yeah, and there's no war on.'

Lordy: 'Oh yes there is. Have you forgotten Putin?'

Fish: 'They'll never get all that gold out of the vaults before the voting is over, and then the people will be in charge and chase the Yanks off home. Even with their Army, and a fleet of helicopters, gold ain't light; how many tons of gold are there? ...

Google it … oh, we can't. Treasure you must know, you work at the Treasury.'

Treasure: 'I need a word with Aristotle. Come with me, Aristotle.'

Treasure and Aristotle moved outside, they stood out of the rain under a shop awning. 'It's me they're after,' said Treasure. 'I have the code to the vaults, they could never smash their way in, there are five of us who each have a component of the code. All five have to be present to gain access to the bullion.'

Aristotle: 'But the time – there's not enough time.'

Treasure: 'There is. Since the 1980s, there has been "Emergency Evacuation" in place, within an hour they can empty the vaults. It's me they're after; you'll have to kill me.'

Aristotle: 'Now, now, there's no need to be so melodramatic, we can hide you in the cellar.'

Treasure: 'Oh yeah, that's the last place they'll look. Nobody ever hid in a cellar.'

Aristotle: 'The police station, if we get you to the police station, they could lock you in a holding cell until 4 p.m., when the revolution would be complete. What I can't quite work out is – who is giving the orders?'

Treasure: 'Yeah, and who's taking orders. And who are controlling the police?'

Aristotle: 'Oh, I take your point – US helicopters, who's running this country? And who exactly is looking for you, the British SAS or the US Delta Force?'

Treasure: 'If we don't get away from here soon, we can ask them, look.' A military vehicle turned the corner; Aristotle dragged Treasure into a shop doorway. A dozen fit young men in training fatigues poured into the pub.

Aristotle pushed on the shop door, it opened. They entered the candlelit tranquillity of a wool shop. Treasure bolted the door and turned the sign to 'Closed'. As their eyes accustomed to the dark, the mother-and-daughter owners appeared from the back of the shop.

In the Albert, a mugshot of Treasure was being flashed around.

The Americans wore balaclavas and said nothing, they pointed and gesticulated showing Treasure's mugshot to the drinkers.

'That's Treasure,' whispered Baldy, 'why do they want Treasure?'

'Where?' asked the soldier from behind his mask.

Baldy: 'I've no idea who it is mate.'

'Where?'

Stick: 'You don't know him. Do you Baldy?'

Baldy: 'Oh, hang on, didn't he used to drink in here? I ain't seen him for ages.'

The American pushed a pistol against Baldy's kneecap. Stick brought his walking stick down across the gun and it discharged harmlessly into the floorboards.

Baldy: 'Fuck you, that could have been dangerous.'

Punch-ups in pubs are not unusual but guns discharging are. Perhaps at the height of any revolution, some form of violence is to be expected but a rootin' tootin' Delta Force squad wasn't placated quite as easily as a few drunken Millwall supporters.

*

They borrowed the shop-owner's car. Aristotle drove and Treasure sat in the back ready to duck down if stopped at a roadblock. However, hiding between the seats with a blanket over him would hardly have fooled the types who were searching for him. They headed for Threadneedle Street and the Bank of England.

Masked militia canvassed the retail outlets neighbouring the Albert. 'Desperate criminal' was their description of Treasure. The mother and daughter in the wool shop gave them the registration number of the car and via short-wave walkie-talkies, the search for Treasure narrowed.

*

There was no definitive evidence of a heist; it was pure speculation and in the absence of a more convincing alternative

– wild speculation. Treasure was unused to excitement on this scale, a game of bridge at the Conservative club was more his measure. The revolution, the impending changes to his life and the lives of his fellow Britons skewed his judgement. *Was the US Delta Force really in pursuit of this little old banger? Was the Bank of England under siege?* Or was there a simpler, more rational explanation?

The only certain way to find out was for Treasure to see for himself. He couldn't delegate the mission because all normal methods of communication were down.

If it were a heist, then the code inside Treasure's head was the missing key to gaining access to the vaults; he should have put as greater distance as possible between his head and the Bank of England – he should have gone south and taken cover in darkest Kent.

*

'What's the time?' asked Aristotle, he looked at the dashboard and answered himself. 'Shit, it's 10.45. Double shit, there's hardly any petrol.'

'Is there enough to get us up town? Do you think the Underground is running? Do they have their own emergency generators?'

'I don't think so. They can't run during a total loss of power.'

The traffic was light, many had taken the day off to follow the voting and celebrate the first day of freedom. There were no traffic lights and this slowed their progress, buses were the only form of public transport.

Aristotle had been analysing the government's actions. 'The one area in which the Tories excel over the new regime is deceit. They have the perfect reasoning – removing the gold reserves to the USA will be explained away as a security precaution in any post-mortem.'

'Oh, you still believe it to be the British government moving the gold to safekeeping? I reckon it's the Yanks stealing it and not

Biden, not the US government. I reckon it's some kind of mafia – Mexican even.'

'God, you could be right.'

They dumped the car in a side street and took a bus. Traffic was eerily quiet, as if London life had been suspended. Low cloud dragged night into mid-morning. There wasn't the usual reflected light from the shop windows; the only illumination came from the headlights of vehicles pushing through the drizzle and reflecting off the black tarmac.

Aristotle: 'Have you any idea where this bus is taking us? Did you see the number?'

Treasure: 'I have no idea, but this road leads towards Westminster – I think. Perhaps we could hide in a pub.'

Aristotle: 'What's our strategy?'

Treasure thought for a while. There was no strategy. He had panicked and followed an impulse to be close to the Bank of England. 'I think we should split up; they'll be looking for two of us. It's stupid to be heading in this direction – I should be heading away from the Bank – as far away as possible. You stay on the bus; I'll get off at the next stop and jump on the next bus going south. Go to the river and check for US military vessels, aircraft carriers that might be waiting to carry the gold away.'

Aristotle: 'And then what do I do? I'm hardly equipped to blow up an aircraft carrier or even report its presence, and who should I report it to, a parking warden?'

Treasure: 'I have a vain hope that the phone network might be the first to be restored. Phone me when you can.'

The magnet that was the Bank of England tugged irresistibly at him, and instead of taking a bus south, Treasure walked in the opposite direction through the back streets towards the Thames. Two green-grey aircraft carriers lay in wait like motionless crocodiles sizing up an unsuspecting gazelle. He gasped, his face flushed and he marched on through the cold.

At last, on the bus alone, Aristotle had time to think. His best thinking time was when he was alone; the thoughts tumbled, they moved slowly along the conveyor belt of his mind. How had they – whoever *they* were, managed to cut the grid so comprehensively. Or was it comprehensive? Was the power cut throughout the whole country? That was the immediate assumption. It might only be London, perhaps the sabotage was solely to enable the stealing of the gold, and had nothing to do with the voting – not political at all, but criminal. Aristotle's reasoning, fuelled by Treasure's revelation about the code to the vaults, led him to believe that the Tory government, jointly with the USA had plotted the heist. America, the heart of capitalism, would suffer most at a successful uprising of the people of Britain. And now rheumatic old Aristotle was the cavalry, his charger was a London bus and his mission was to stop the USA running off with the entire UK gold reserves. He burst into laughter; *how on earth had Baldy hit upon the ridiculous idea that there was a plot to steal the national gold reserves. How did Baldy's brain work?*

Aristotle walked into a police station.

'So, you want to report a robbery. Have you been mugged, or had your car stolen?'

'You won't believe what I'm about to tell you.'

'Oh, my gawd, I wish I had a fiver for every time I'd heard that opening sentence.'

'There is an attempt to rob the Bank of England.'

'Then it ain't the police you want – try 007.'

'What do you think all those helicopters are doing? The USA is trying to get into the vaults of the Bank of England and steal the country's gold reserves.'

'And what evidence do you have? Those helicopters are trying to sort out the power failure; at least, that's what I've been told, although I must admit an electrician would seem more appropriate.'

'Look, you must take me seriously. Do you have an officer who can accompany me to Threadneedle Street and take a look?'

'Okay sir, you don't seem the type to cry wolf, and I'm due for a break so I'll take a stroll with you to see what's happening. It's a weird day, what with the vote, and the end of the world, and people stuck in lifts, so why not President Biden robbing the Bank of England.'

The area around the Bank was cordoned off. Armed militia, similar to the ones back at the pub, stood around in their dozens.

Sergeant: ''Ello, 'ello, 'ello, what's goin' on 'ere, then?'

Aristotle: 'I can't believe you said that.'

Sergeant: 'I say? Who's in charge?'

There was no reaction. Aristotle heard mumbling, the tight-lipped Americans were clearly reacting to the sight of a London bobby with three stripes on his arm. They waved the sergeant through but blocked Aristotle's way when he tried to follow. The sergeant was led away and out of sight.

Aristotle heard raised voices, not quite shouting but a disagreement between two of the men. He could not distinguish the words … and when he realised why not, he took a step back, and when he heard the muffled sound of a discharging pistol … he took another step back, turned and, despite having not broken into more than a trot for a decade or more – ran. The words he had heard were Russian.

*

'I want to report a murder!' This had quite a different response back at the police station and Aristotle was taken to an interview room. He told the officer what had happened.

'A sergeant? From this station? Ten minutes ago?'

'Yes, and you'd better call out the Army.'

The highest-ranking officer at the station was a detective chief superintendent. There were now eight people focused on Aristotle. 'When I give you the nod, tell us again what has happened. We will record everything you say on our private phones, while the batteries hold out. Are you ready?'

Aristotle gave his name, and told them that he was a retired welder from Greenwich. 'I thought they were US Delta Force until I heard them speaking Russian. The helicopters display USA livery, but they ain't Americans, they're bloody Russians – and I wouldn't be surprised if there are ships or submarines waiting on the Thames to carry off the gold.'

'But how do they plan to breach security?'

'Don't ask me, I have no idea.' Aristotle had begun to trust no one. He certainly wasn't willing to implicate Treasure.

'You need to focus on your sergeant, I heard a shot … it might be too late.'

'How many Russians – if they are Russians – do you reckon there are?'

'I saw about eighteen or twenty, but I couldn't see inside the building – or the other side, there could quite easily be forty or fifty.'

'And we are only eight, and your suggestion to call out the Army was sound advice, but we can't call anyone. We need ambulances as well, but they won't come until the situation is secure, even if we could call them.'

'So, what are you going to do, sit around waiting for the electricity to come back on?'

'We need to discuss the matter, we're somewhat hamstrung at the moment.'

'Hamstrung? What about your sergeant?'

'Thanks for your help. We've sent a runner, quite literally, for an electrician to fix the emergency generator. When that is working, we'll have electricity and we can make you a nice cup of tea. Show the gentleman to room 7.'

Two constables escorted Aristotle to a cell and slammed the self-locking door behind him.

*

Treasure had circumnavigated the whole of the Threadneedle Street area. He wore a Covid facemask and drew no special attention. If apprehended, he had sworn to himself not to give up the code. He looked at his watch 11.04. There was nothing the man could do. He was tempted to go to his office at the Treasury but was certain it would be under surveillance. The aircraft carriers moored on the Thames indicated how the gold would be transported across the Atlantic Ocean.

Aristotle banged on the iron door and shouted. The police officers held their meeting.

'What about Sarge, do you think he's dead?'

'No chance. Sarge knew what he was doing; it was a bluff to frighten off old matey, the welder.'

'It certainly worked, but we are in a fix. Our orders are not to react to the relocation of the gold reserves unless the revolution is voted in. So 3 p.m. at the very latest.'

'How do you work that out?'

'All the votes should be in by 4 p.m., that's the cut-off point, and they said that once they have all the security codes to hand, it only takes an hour to empty the vaults.'

'It's coming up to 11.30 so there's loads of time. We just have to keep the welder bloke out of the way and bide our time. And when the new government is eventually voted in ...'

'There's no way that's gonna happen,' sniggered a young constable.

'I voted for it,' said a colleague.

'So did I,' said another.

'But we were instructed to vote against.'

'Democracy, mate – I voted *for* as well. No one tells me how to vote. We might be coppers but we are free citizens, too. And if this revolution gets voted through, we'll have a new government, of which we will be a part. This raid on the Bank of England will be considered the apex of Tory corruption and deceit. And there's a risk we'll be accused of being complicit.'

'It's not a raid you idiot, it's moving the gold bullion to safety ...'

'Ever been had? Russian-speaking Yanks with their hands on the country's gold! I'm certain the USA hasn't started recruiting Russians into their army.'

'Blimey, what do we do? So, who voted *for* and who voted *against*?' The three who were qualified to vote, all voted *for*.

'I would have voted *for*, too. We were told the gold would be moved to America for safekeeping, to keep it away from the communist uprising. It's all a bunch of lies. We've been lied to – again. Putin is nicking our gold from right under our noses! Britain will be the laughing stock of the world if he gets away with it!'

*

The Tories knew that if they were overthrown by the people, the new government's manifesto would trigger the beginning of the end of capitalism. The American administration and, more importantly, the tight-knit group of conglomerate leaders who controlled the world economy feared it, too. Direct democracy alone would only hinder their control – the press and media would still be able manipulate the malleable minds of the consumer; but without money, without currency, capitalism would be dead.

The panicked Tory government had failed to negotiate the cooperation of the Biden administration. Putin, desperate for funds for armaments, agreed to *take care* of the gold reserves. The Tories' last-ditch tactic to scupper the revolution was to impoverish the nation, thereby severing trade connections abroad. They would, of course, claim the Russians had the gold in safekeeping until normality returned. The nebulous leaders of the revolution would be brought to book, and a wounded British government, perhaps a coalition, would try to earn the sympathy of the world and gain their support in recovering their gold from Putin.

This strategy was, of course, flawed on all fronts. Putin was a universally recognised pariah. No legitimate government would enter into negotiations of any description with that man. To blame the leaders of the revolution for the loss of the gold was also pointless – there were no leaders – and to load the blame onto the entire British population resembled the abandoned plot of a Gilbert and Sullivan comic opera.

Treasure had so far successfully moved from one hiding place to another. The code in his head which had the potential to cost Britain its entire gold reserves – remained there. The clock ticked – and the hands on the clock face of Big Ben moved through 4 p.m. – the original cut-off time for voting. Treasure was certain that the last of the live votes had been cast hours before. Had any online votes been possible? Perhaps there were parts of the country unaffected by the power cut.

*

The gaffer tape was ripped from the sergeant's mouth and he was left to call for help.

The Russians made their retreat – time was up and they began their withdrawal; they packed up their equipment and the helicopters joined the aircraft carriers.

*

Gradually, to avoid dangerous surges, electricity was restored to the grid. Communication became normalised – Aristotle was liberated from the holding cell and he immediately phoned Treasure who watched from a bench overlooking the river as Putin's aircraft carriers wended their way eastward along the Thames towards the estuary.

*

Aristotle and Treasure sat by the hearth in the warmth of a riverside pub, they enjoyed hot tea with a whisky chaser. The online voting deadline had been extended to 7 p.m. The screen at the bar showed that the *for* votes were well ahead. 'Have you voted?' smiled Aristotle.

'Oops, been a tad distracted.' Treasure voted on his mobile phone and watched the numbers counting upwards in their millions. 'So, it must have been a countrywide power cut.'

'Must have been, and it can only have helped boost the *for* vote.'

Treasure nodded, 'Especially among the *don't knows*.'

*

The power cut had delayed the voting, but the screen in the pub showed the results from the live parliaments and it was clear that the new government would be voted in and, at 7 p.m., the final results were announced, 85 per cent *for* and 11 per cent *against* with a few *don't knows*.

At 8.15 a piercing screech from the western sky signalled the approach of four RAF jet fighters. The new government of the people had already issued its first command and the jets escorted Putin's aircraft carriers – bereft of gold bars – until they were clear of British waters.

*

The months and weeks leading up to Day Zero had seen huge volumes of money leaving Britain.

Foreigners and Brits exchanged their pounds for dollars and euros. With each passing hour, the weakening pound bought less of the chosen currency. Foreign nationals transferred money to their home countries. If post-revolution life in Britain proved too austere, they had a safe alternative and would follow their money home. The mortally wounded Tory government did nothing to reverse or slow the decline – rabbits in headlights, spite, or plain inertia – no one knew. The Labour Party was strangely silent; many members openly favoured the revolution but most held their cards close to their chest. If the revolution failed, they might be able to resurrect their political career.

But the revolution did not fail, it was a resounding success and as a result the pound sterling suddenly looked a cheeky outsider for those traders around the world willing to chance their arm.

Part Two

Day Zero – The Albert Pub,
18 January 2023, 7 p.m.

Lordy: 'There's pie and chips, and sausage and mash with onion gravy; help yourselves.'

Champagne corks popped and the beer flowed. The lights were dimmed and cigar smoke danced on candle-wax thermals like the tormented spirits of a dead past.

Baldy: 'Blimey, talk about living in the land of plenty.'

Lordy: 'Yeah, milk and honey tomorrow, as long as the deliveries arrive.'

They ate, drank and celebrated freedom.

Lordy: 'Washing up in the kitchen, volunteers, please.'

*

In another part of London work had already begun on the top priority – homelessness.

Julia

Blue cigarette smoke wafted from slits cut in the sides of a tumble-dryer box. The occupant was a petite woman in her early twenties; she exchanged warmth with a mongrel pup nestled in her embrace inside a tatty old sleeping bag. A row of her possessions was carefully arranged against the blackened red-brick wall of the railway arch, a French-knitting bobbin, a plastic yellow rose on a long stalk, a goldfish in a jar, a single grubby satin ballet shoe, an unopened packet of crisps well past its best-before date, a Christmas-tree bauble with a hole in it and an empty picture frame.

'Hello, is anyone home?'

'Woof,' came a startled puppy woof; although it was *boof* more than woof.

'Who is it? Go away, I have nothing worth nicking.'

'We have a warm flat for you, a comfortable bed and food. And we'll get a basket for your dog.'

'Bloody do-gooders,' she never meant them to hear it, it was a thought, but in her doped state, thought was often indistinguishable from speech.

'We can drive you there now.' The woman was helped from her cardboard box to an awaiting van. Her possessions were carefully packed down and put in the back.

'I haven't any money for rent.' She was well spoken and articulate with an economic use of words.

'Don't worry, how are you?' Her face was gaunt and showed signs of malnourishment. She still wore her sleeping bag, she'd cut holes for her feet and it hid a bruised, abused body of skin and bone.

Her two female rescuers showed her into the flat. 'Here's the kitchen I'll put the kettle on, tea or coffee?'

'Tea. Who are you? Thanks.'

'Are you aware of the new government?'

'I have no interest in politics or politicians, they're all charlatans.' She sat cross-legged on a sofa and held her puppy close, drinking her tea and feeding the dog digestive biscuits.

'We can pop to the shops and get a basket and some dog food, what does she eat?'

'I've got no money to pay for all this. What does my dog eat? She eats my leftovers – which isn't much.'

'I'll get some puppy food, how old is she?'

'Who are you?'

'Let me explain ...'

'So, your story is that the Tories have been voted out, money doesn't exist any more, and the people of Britain are running the country via an app. Do you really expect me to believe this? You'll be telling me next Vladimir Putin is Santa Claus and the prime minister is Che Guevara.'

'It's only just happened, yesterday, Day Zero, and we're trying to house everyone. Look, here's a Pyrex dish, we can put your goldfish in here; even he won't be sleeping rough tonight.'

'Don't take me for stupid; you want to get me sectioned. Then I'll be out of sight and out of mind – much better for tourism ...'

'Look, kid, wise up, this is real. I know you don't believe me but while you have been hiding away in your cardboard box a revolution has taken place. This block of flats is owned – was owned – by a Chinese investment company. It is now owned by the people of Britain – you are a person who needs somewhere to live – just accept it! Get a shower and we can go shopping. What do you reckon – an aquarium or a round goldfish bowl? If we go for an aquarium we could add more goldfish to keep him company. Do you have a mobile?'

They walked in the dark to the shops. Julia told of her childhood ambition to be a ballet dancer and the rescuer outlined the ambitions of the new Great Britain.

Julia wrote on the app for the first time. 'This stupid, weak person was rescued from the streets by two kind women. They put me in a flat, gave me food, talked to me, listened to me, fed my dog, walked my dog, re-housed my goldfish, and gave me a laptop, shopping card and phone. *Rich girl from the sticks seeks excitement in London*. Well, I certainly found it. Booze, drugs – yes, I lived the cliché. Enterprising pushers picked up on the signals and this naive eager-to-please babe was sold. This app is a serious forum and not a shoulder to cry on, and I'm not crying, not any more. Respect to the revolutionary British people for putting up with wimps like me. I promise to live my life in the spirit of the revolution and dance and dance and dance.'

*

Back at the pub Lordy read from the app: 'I sit in a position of command at the Ministry of Defence. It looks like the prime minister has done a bunk and now my government is you, the people of Britain, and I take my orders from you. There is war in Europe. A critical aspect of war is secrecy – which isn't provided for on this app. I understand the importance of openness and transparency, but quite the opposite is essential in matters of war and defence. Please discuss and advise.'

Stick: 'Is he calling for a secret app?'

Baldy: 'Secrecy don't seem right, it's not proper democracy, if you know what I mean. There ain't supposed to be secrets; that was agreed, it's all meant to be open and honest.'

Lee: 'I know what you mean Baldy, but say for example the MoD wanted to send an SAS sniper to Russia to assassinate Putin, it would hardly help if they first debated it in an open forum with sixty million people.'

Stick: 'But nor can you give a green light to taking out the head of state of another country, even if it probably would be approved by the majority of Brits; the majority of the rest of the planet, too. What do you think Aristotle?'

Aristotle: 'It's an interesting conundrum, there are theme-specific apps popping up all over the place, sports apps in particular, but they're not locked, anyone can see what's going on. A secret app might be approved if it was monitored by a small number of trustees but, as Baldy said, that would go against the spirit of the revolution. It might be an idea to rewrite the Ministry of Defence's brief in the manifesto and rename it the Ministry of Defence and Attack.'

Baldy: 'Is this conversation official government business?'

Fish: 'How do you mean?'

Baldy: 'I realise that Lee was just using the assassination of Putin as an example, but would it end the war? Or would it make matters worse?'

Fish: 'No, not that, you asked if this was government business. What did you mean?'

Baldy: 'Well, last week, pre-revolution, we were simple citizens chatting in a pub, and now, post-revolution, we are parliamentarians discussing important matters as if we were government ministers. Which, in a way, is what we are; that's what I mean … is this government business or a bit of idle chinwagging?'

Aristotle: 'Profound, profound, you do come up with some gems sometimes Baldy. Your comment illustrates perfectly how our attitude has to change – has changed – in your case.'

Baldy blushed.

Aristotle: 'Secrecy is central in the business of spying and the dark arts of international diplomacy. Secrecy and intelligence are the diplomat's bread and butter.'

Baldy: 'Chucking bombs over the neighbour's fence ain't exactly diplomatic. Putin needs one up the rectum. Diplomacy never stopped war – war stops war.'

Aristotle: 'Propaganda is an efficient and less bloody weapon. If the UK revolution is seen abroad as a success and if the Russian people become aware of what is possible, they might topple Putin. And they are the people who should deal with him – the Russian people, not a foreign assassin.'

Lordy: 'So what's it gonna be Baldy, diplomacy or Exocet rectal irrigation?'

Lee: 'You need to be careful; even talk of the assassination of Putin could unite the Russian people and escalate the war. And on the other hand, an unsuccessful assassination attempt might result in a nuclear warhead landing on London.'

Fish: 'We're getting away from the point – what are we going to put on the app?'

Stick: 'You're right, Fish. So, instead of a Ministry of Defence, a Ministry of Propaganda – or perhaps a Ministry of Information would sound better.'

Treasure: 'Renaming a government department is pointless. It will require a series of citizens' assemblies covering defence and security.'

Baldy: 'I don't see the point of any country attacking us. Money causes wars. And we've got no money, see, and that's why people fight wars.'

Lee: 'Now don't push it, Baldy. There are still the gold reserves, although I think it will be a long time before there's another raid on the Bank of England.'

Stick: 'And Putin's war is nothing to do with money, it's power and nostalgia for his beloved Soviet Union. Just like old Adolf in the Second World War – you'd think people would learn, wouldn't you?'

Lee: 'Psychopaths, it's always psychopaths …'

This is what they agreed to put on the app:

'This is a matter for citizens' assemblies; the UK government should start as it means to carry on. Old-school political parties have often promised *openness and transparency* – a promise invariably broken. Established departments like the MoD must change their thinking; direct democracy is a different style of management. Foreign regimes will quickly learn that a country not managed by politicians doesn't lie. Secrecy is a form of deceit and the people of Britain should not have to tolerate deceit as a tool of government.'

Many contributors on the app warmed to the idea of a series of citizens' assemblies to tackle the issue.

*

During the first week of liberty – as it was being called, public transport ran normally, children went to school and people in essential jobs went to work. Even accountants, bankers and all those employed in fields associated with money turned up at the office – despite there being no pay cheque at the end of the month. Companies had to be wound down, books had to balance, and legal contracts had to be terminated professionally. Many people suspected – some hoped – that the time would come when the revolution faltered and collapsed, that files would be dusted off and normality would return.

All banks were closed for business on 18 January, Day Zero – they never opened their doors again.

Innately tidy chief accountants at bank head offices worked frantically to balance the books. Due to the practice of fractional reserve banking, all banks ended their final day of trading with massive deficits. This was not deemed at all strange to the banking world, there was no admonition, no shame. Lopsided closing accounts were wholly the result of the death of money. The trail of each pound deficit would lead to mortgages and eventually bricks and mortar – homes – and there the trail would end.

Ledger files would close and collect dust, they were, after all only numbers on paper. A new set of accounts was about to open and the reckoning would be in human happiness – environmental consideration – humility – the arts and assisting other nations to follow the example set by Great Britain.

The only non-Ponzi, non-fiat currency on the planet was the UK pound. Sterling had the backing of 310 tonnes of gold reserves. The price of gold had rocketed. Uncertainty caused by the turbulence in the world money markets saw countries outbidding each other for the precious metal. The resurrection of the UK pound as a viable currency had begun.

The British people shone a floodlight which exposed a *money-based economy* as redundant and *representative democracy* as a confidence trick and a pathway for psychopaths to pursue their dictatorial ambitions.

Bright light however was overkill; the cold January sun was quite sufficient illumination, and as daylight hours lengthened and spring beckoned, *the truth of the new* formed buds alongside the snowdrops.

Ireland was becoming familiar with the app and the people of Poland, Greece, Mexico and Italy requested their own versions of the app. Under the directive of the British people, work on making the app available to any county which requested it was approved.

*

The Royal Navy had orders from the new British government to intercept dinghies crammed with illegal immigrants on their way to the south coast and tow them safely back to French waters. But the threat alone put a stop to the boats. The perception of a 'non-bluff' British government was already emerging. Honesty – the antithesis of politics – was evolving as an important tool.

No more dinghies left French beaches and none were ever intercepted under this directive. Perhaps a Britain without money was less attractive to migrants.

*

There was now freedom of speech and skeletons in cupboards were aired on the app – multiculturalism – homelessness – what to do with genuine asylum seekers – the treatment of Muslim women by Muslim men (a debate initiated by thousands of Muslim women) were all legitimate debates to be had, and they were on the agenda.

On the app: 'Multiculturalism might be renamed *enhanced conflictism* were it not so clunky. When conflict within families under the same roof is rampant, and conflict within the same religion causes wars – how can anyone believe that harmony can be created by mixing cultures which are diametrically opposed? The term "multiculturalism" is misleading: culture – the arts – the humanities – it would indeed be wonderful if multiculturalism worked – but it rarely does.

'The social engineers who promoted multiculturalism aren't easily identified – surely it wasn't the BBC alone. But whoever it was, opened a Pandora's Box and sneaked away without claiming responsibility.

'Perhaps conflict is okay and perhaps harmony is overrated. I hope this new government isn't going to sweep awkward problems such as multiculturalism under the carpet.'

*

Homelessness was tackled that cold January evening of Day Zero. Not everyone was off the streets, but by the following evening every homeless person was in the warm.

The backlog of illegal immigrants and asylum seekers was considerably reduced when individuals were offered a 'no questions asked' one-way ticket home. Those genuine asylum seekers were grouped into their nationalities and interviewed individually by a sympathetic panel. Under the new regime there was now plenty of manpower to achieve this.

They were asked: 'What do you want from Britain? What can you offer Britain? Where on this planet would you prefer to live? How can the situation in your home country be influenced to make it safe for you to return?'

Every asylum seeker had their skills and qualifications recorded. A file was compiled with their story and their reason for being in Britain.

The revolution, the moneyless economy and direct democracy were explained to them. 'Would your native land benefit from similar changes?'

Details were gathered of the criminal agents paid to transport them to Britain. A dossier was building of a complex network of criminal gangs.

Islam and the treatment of Muslim women by their men would fill much of the debate over the next few months.

Winners – Losers; direct democracy doesn't magically cleanse the population of stupidity. Stupidity and ignorance are inherent in all regimes and always will be. With every new statute there are winners and losers. The winners are not automatically more worthy than the losers. Rational argument isn't always the magic key – sometimes it's simply the majority that wins. How would the losers be appeased – if at all? Legislation would have to be written into the constitution. Citizens' assemblies would be set up and their recommendations voted on.

*

And so to Northern Ireland, a country born of the cruel actions of the British ruling class.

The 1.9 million population of this region, 46 per cent Catholics, 43 per cent Protestants and 11 per cent others (including twelve thousand Muslims) voted *for* the revolution, but only just.

The Protestant contingent had always suspected the revolution to be 'reunification by the back door'. They either couldn't grasp or didn't believe that there would be no formal government of the traditional model – that *they* were now the government.

Vigorous debate on the app in the Republic pointed to the *back door* being ajar. Preparations for seventy-eight 'live' nationwide parliaments were underway; the appointed date was Wednesday, 1 March 2023.

There were those in Northern Ireland who somehow lacked the fresh thinking required to accept this new type of government. How could the Conservative hard-liners who had voted *against* be appeased? Opinion on the app was divided. One school of thought leaned towards offering them homes in mainland Britain. This could easily be achieved; there were plenty of decent houses abandoned by those who had fled the country and second homes brought into common ownership. Others backed the idea that now was the time to show the brutal reality of the 'winner–loser' aspect of direct democracy. Should the stance be: 'tough, this is direct democracy, argue your case on the app and get on with life –you are the government – stop moaning and govern!'

There was, however a growing belief that the border would go the way of the Berlin Wall and that the Republic of Ireland would leave Europe, become united with the north and that the whole of Ireland would adopt a moneyless economy, direct democracy and self-government.

There was the temptation to extrapolate the concept – to dare to dream of a United British Isle – then a United Europe – and from there to a united – oh well, let's not get too far ahead of ourselves.

The UK would battle on and wait for the result of the voting in the Republic on 1 March.

*

Activity – on and off the app, 21 January 2023.

Money was a thing of the past in the United Kingdom – deceitful politicians were a thing of the past, and as the fog cleared many of the problems of the past faded with it. New problems of course manifested, and old familiar ones remained – hospital waiting lists – dirty river water, etc.

But an infrastructure was building to deal with these situations. Kicked into touch were budgets and party politics. Manipulative psychopaths had been neutered and the new body of voters allowed themselves a little swagger.

Across the board, children, teenagers, adults and the elderly had a clearer sight of their aims. Money, no longer stood in the way, careers were not straightjackets. If a youngster had a passion for football, they could play all the football they liked, they could join a club; get tactical training, fitness in the gym and play in serious matches in a league. Their day was balanced with school lessons and work. Happy boys and girls played their football – for fun not money.

News channels reported the news minus the hysterical spin demanded by advertisers. The news was often about local meetings in community halls; on the agenda – dirty rivers, anti-social behaviour, illegal immigrants, noise, schools, Scout huts and the needs of the elderly. Foreign news was like a mirror of Britain's past; power struggles, the economy – inflation and poverty.

The new style government was in place – it had been talked about and speculated on in pubs, in homes and the workplace and now the people's government had arrived, it was real, and it was here. It was Marley's ghost, with chains falling at every step – it was corsets snapping their ties – it was that deep forbidden sigh – it was freedom and it was joyous.

The Stepladder

A man walked into a café. He was clean-shaven, mid-forties and sensibly dressed against the cold. Paracetamols rattled against the glass bottle in his pocket. The parade of shops was familiar to him but he hadn't been in the café before. A menu chalked on a blackboard caught his eye and he looked at it blankly, seeing but not reading.

It was a well-established café from the 1940s, plenty of shiny chrome and mirrors. It had survived the Wimpy Bar craze and, more recently, the burger craze. An Italian had started it just after the war and the current incumbents (not owners, of course) were descendants.

'There are pickles on the counter. Aren't you from the bank?' asked hairy armed Miguel as he brought him a cheese sandwich and cup of tea.

'Yes, I am the chief cashier, was chief cashier – out of work layabout now I'm afraid.'

'Oh, you'll find something; it takes time to adjust; it's been a tremendous upheaval. But no more banks, eh?' Miguel was in his fifties and the loosely fitting apron around his waist signalled too much pasta and too little exercise. He served another customer then returned to the chief cashier's table. 'May I?'

'Certainly, sit down, how are you finding it? It must be strange not taking money over the counter.'

'Well, it is strange, but I think it's going to be good for the country. The café was doing fine before, financially we were stable, high council tax and business rates were a pain, but we had no debt and we took a lot of cash you understand, so no real stress. We had a setback two years ago when we were robbed, hooded thugs walked in, baseball bats, one of them had a knife, the café was full, the till was full – I put up a fight – still got the scars – but they still waltzed out with the contents of the till.'

'Yeah, I read about it in the paper. That's a horrible thing to have happened.'

'It was, I considered shutting shop, but you can't let things like that beat you. I guess armed robbery is a thing of the past now.'

'Yes, I suppose it is. One would certainly hope so. I'd never considered that to be an aspect of the revolution. I didn't think it would be voted in, quite honestly; I didn't want it to happen. I'm outside the voting range and so could only argue against it on the app. So, will you stay open?'

'So long as I can get the ingredients I will. What's the point of closing down. People need somewhere to get a bite to eat, a cup of coffee and a chat. And it means I can make some changes to the menu – still do the sandwiches and snacks, but experiment with proper cooking – exotic Italian dishes *justa like Mama used to make*, if you know what I mean.'

'Ha, you sound very positive. I wish I could see a silver lining, but people don't need banks any more. You know, it's weird. It's all weird, but there's something specific that I find most peculiar – quaintly English I suppose.'

'What's that?'

'There's no pressure. They don't put any pressure on you to get a job. I don't think they care.'

'Who are *they*?'

'Pardon?'

'There is no *they*. There is no big stick to beat you with. It used to be that if you didn't send off enough job applications, they'd stop your benefits. But now there's no *they* – no *them and us* – and there are no benefits. *They* are me. *They* are the two mums in corner over there. *They* are you.'

'Self-discipline; is that what you mean?'

'Not really. No, that's not what I meant, but take that if you will. It's early days; you need time to think.'

He thanked his host, and handed him his shopping card, chuckled and left the café. Across from the parade of shops was the common where kids played football and cricket. He crossed the road, leaned against the iron rail and surveyed the row of shops. He patted the tablets in his pocket. There was the café, and to the left, Bob's the DIY shop where, after the war, probably at the same time the café opened, they'd sell paraffin and nails. To the right was Sister's Salon the ladies' hairdresser. Steam condensed on the inside of the window and water collected in white towels on the window ledge.

The shops hadn't changed since the revolution, or at least he thought as much. He knew the parade, and popped into the mini-supermarket from time to time.

Outside Bob's shop was the usual display of bags of compost, plastic buckets, a wheelbarrow filled with left-footed wellington boots (he asked Bob about that once – it was in case of theft – the police would be able to focus on a narrower list of one-legged suspects) trowels, hoes, garden forks and the stepladder. Ha ha, the wooden stepladder had been there for ages – they had metal ones at B&Q at half the price. He was sure Bob gave it the occasional lick of wood preserver to tone it up, but it had never sold – and now it was too late. Something else struck him. There had always been a blue plastic-covered steel-cable intricately woven in and out of the wheelbarrow axle, anywhere it could secure the bigger items – the rungs of the stepladder, too. Bob had abandoned it, of course: everything was free. There was no need for security.

The chief cashier smiled, it looked the same but it wasn't. It was different, very different. They were all open for business but it wasn't business they were open for – they were just open.

The restaurateur was a parliamentarian, Bob was a parliamentarian, and the hairdresser was a parliamentarian. Mr Patel at the mini-supermarket was a parliamentarian. *He* was a parliamentarian for God's sake. They were in charge of this country – it was their country. The chief cashier suddenly felt overwhelmingly safe. His world shed all the uncertainty that had made him sneak the paracetamol into his pocket and leave the house with no plans to return. From being unsure, frightened even, his world flipped. Within those few seconds everything changed – the sun shone – well, it didn't actually; it started raining cats and dogs.

He hid his face, turned his back and looked across the common. He covered his mouth with his hand and looked up to the sky. He couldn't stop the tears, his shoulders gyrated and the raindrops splashed onto his face mingling with the falling tears. He was safe.

*

A week later, on his way to the café, he noticed that the stepladder had gone. He'd become a regular at the café, helping to wash-up in the kitchen when he had the time. He arranged with the proprietor for a surprise birthday party for his daughter, who was six in a fortnight. When the time arrived, the stepladder was back in its usual place.

Over the coming months, on his way to college on the bus (he was training to be an electrician), he noticed that the stepladder was sometimes leaning against the wall and at other times, for days, it was gone.

'Aha, I've changed a few things,' said Bob when asked about the stepladder. 'Customers now borrow tools and equipment rather than own them. My storage shed out the back is open all hours and the accountants down the road have written a programme so that people register what they are using and when they are expecting to return them – clever, eh? And we'll soon need more storage space because of donations. Instead of cement mixers and barbecues crowding out people's garages they are centralised here for everyone to use.'

'But isn't that a bit inconvenient, I mean if you want a barbecue and have to fetch it from here?'

'Delivery,' said Bob triumphantly, 'we have a delivery rota, it works like this. You are registered within the system and when you want to use, say a cement mixer – we have three to choose from – it is delivered in good time. A spin-off – spin-off – cement mixer – ha ha – is that you might be lucky enough to be offered a helping hand with your building project. People have more time nowadays. Would you like to register?'

*

Inquisitive individuals around the world were familiarising themselves with the app. They watched events unfold in the UK and imagined life in their country under a similar regime.

They received news of the developments in Britain from their establishment-based broadcasting agencies, but a more reliable source came from friends and relations in the UK via messaging, email and chats over the telephone. This information was authentic, it was unspun – the good and the bad.

The European Union in particular faced severe examination. What if member nations began to follow Britain's lead?

International trade was functioning smoothly; if the UK bought goods from a company in Spain, for example, it was paid directly from the Bank of England. And if the UK sold goods to a Spanish firm the reverse would happen. There were measurable deficits/surpluses. But Britain's trading partners would have to make hay – the UK was keen to be self-sufficient – especially in foodstuffs, even if this meant being weaned off exotic fare. It was dawning on people that the desire for fashionable dishes had been driven by advertising. Plainer, healthier eating with seasonable home-grown fruit and vegetables was to become the norm. The absence of strawberries off-season made them something to look forward to. Strawberries returned to being a summer treat – jams and ice cream a winter teaser.

Manufactures abroad were threatened by UK sustainable products flooding their markets. It was bound to put them out of business; 'designed obsolescence' had no place in a moneyless economy. And the worry reached beyond the manufacturers – a fall in turnover and thereby tax revenues threatened to undermine economies of the old style.

As the weeks passed, the British people began to realise just what an influence money had had pre-revolution. Gone was the constant marketing: television – computer – mobile phones – cold calling – social media – newspapers and magazines; everything from a milk bottle to a neon sign had been a vehicle for advertising. That ghastly element of life had vanished, and *contagious, hypnotic suggestibility* – meat and drink for advertisers, reverted to a quaint human characteristic.

Local street markets still functioned; fruit and veg, the coffee stall, cakes and sandwiches, pies and pasties were all still available. Most of the stallholders carried on as usual, working the local markets was a lifestyle and a social event as well as a way of making a living. And now it was a social event and a public service.

Their friends were here, their friends and fellow parliamentarians. The post-revolution changes were widely accepted, but everything was happening so fast and there was a need to slow down. It was recognised that some traditions should be maintained for the sake of those unsettled by the change. The handbrake was applied locally by parliamentarians in response to what was, after all, a nebulous signal. There was no need for old-style social engineering by a disconnected local county council – no words – no meetings – just simple self-governing. And so the market traders carried on as normal.

Stallholders were more relaxed, everything was free. Customers swiped their shopping cards and took only what they needed, why would they take more? What would be the point? There would be another market tomorrow with more fresh fruit.

In supermarkets, space had been cleared for tables and chairs so that people could sit and drink a cup of tea and eat a cream bun from the shelves. People could peruse the app and watch the news on what was happening in Poland, Greece, Mexico, Ireland and Italy. They chuckled at the German chancellor and French president trying to keep a lid on the crippled system in Europe. They watched subtitled broadcasts of rioting Frenchmen, striking workers across the whole continent of Europe, and listened to politicians lying to stay in power. They saw room-sized graphs in European television studios with energetic journalists pointing. 'Here we have inflation – this is interest rates and here is the projected interest rate ... proving the necessity for growth!'

*

Pubs initially saw an increase in drunkenness and the associated problem of violence. But behaviour gradually became more civilised as the app directed that those found to be drunk and disorderly would spend three days and nights in the prison (rather than in A&E) under medical supervision. The same drunks complained on the app that their human rights had been breached. An overwhelming response reminded them of their own 'human responsibilities' and that their inconsiderate behaviour had no doubt impinged the 'human rights' of others. The message was clear, *behave in a civilised manner*.

But there was disorder of another type, and it was most surprising. There were those who took their responsibility as parliamentarians to another level. Even something as trivial as dropping litter would see these zealots confronting the miscreants, elderly women brandishing rolled-up umbrellas and insisting the young men pick up the cigarette packet. Schoolchildren abandoned the universally understood anti-squealing code and were known to report speeding motorists together with pictures of number plates. The same motorists reported the kids for throwing stones at their speeding cars.

A request on the app called for an end to this vigilantism.

*

On the app: 'An investigation should be launched into the attempted removal of the gold reserves. Those responsible should be brought to account.'

On the app: 'I agree that there should an investigation but many of the suspects have left the country. The revolution has exposed the old-style politics as an environment where such dishonourable conduct is inevitable. To their credit, many former politicians are vocal on the app and have embraced the people's government.

'There is no need for spiteful retribution, rather take a leaf out of Nelson Mandela's book, and forgive.'

*

A survey of dwellings began. A report on the condition of every house and flat was to be completed. South-facing rooves were earmarked for solar panels and a home-insulation programme was prioritised. A recruitment drive into the building industry was launched with apprenticeships available for candidates of all ages. The term *dead occupations* arose, it encompassed all money-churning, money-counting activities, including sales and marketing, advertising, insurance, accounting, tax-collecting, etc.

Housing estates, villages, towns and cities were analysed – people were interviewed and their suggestions on how life could be improved were noted. An emergency housing app was launched where people in poor housing could request help. Existing council housing officers were often in the know and their experience was vital. New build, it transpired, was rarely the answer.

The practice of wealthy city dwellers buying up housing stock for their holiday homes in attractive resorts was being reversed. Everybody would have a home – one home. Second homes were no longer an option; locals had been priced out of the housing market and now dwellings that were occupied two or three weeks of the year were available to house local young families.

In the new economy, there was no clamour to concrete over farmland – quite the reverse. Surplus buildings would be demolished, lawns would be laid and, where appropriate, long-term wilding projects would be established. Oaks and beech trees would grow alongside holly and spruce.

Redundant buildings were carefully assessed and either converted or demolished. Bricks and reusable materials were categorised, recorded and stored appropriately; they were made available to anyone anywhere in the country. The aim was to stop brick production and reduce tree felling. The larger plots, where collections of undesirable or unnecessary buildings once stood were converted into sports fields and parks – or allotments for local food production. Where possible, nature reserves were linked to establish uninterrupted wildlife networks.

Education was pulled apart, analysed and reassembled; children would have a unique tailor-made education (as in *A World without Money or Politicians*). It was considered important to balance – the assimilation of facts – appreciating the arts – and creativity. Each child would be coached in singing and encouraged to play at least one musical instrument.

Children would not only study, they would work as well, a few hours a week, depending on the child. This was their Britain and as much their responsibility as any adult. And there would be play – play – and more play.

Adults could take sabbaticals and there would be study modules; everyone would be encouraged to study to completion as many modules as possible.

Those wanting employment and those with vacancies met on a dedicated app and just got on with it.

It was a breathless, frantic period of British history.

*

On the app: 'Because professional football is no longer an option in this country, I would like to get together with some football enthusiasts to reorganise the structure of soccer. My son plays for the local club and hopes to continue but the whole future of the game needs to be restructured.'

*

In order to open up space on the original app, specialised apps were springing up; especially for sport: association football, cricket, rugby – all sports would have their local leagues to feed regional leagues and ultimately a national elite league of top players.

Gemma and Oscar

'We should have gone months ago; I've stashed over twenty grand in cash so that we could start again in Spain and now they've abolished money. What are we gonna do? I'm finished.'

'Now come and sit down, Oscar.' The twenty-year-olds sat on the settee. 'You are not finished; this is an opportunity to start again. No more going out at night breaking into people's garages and nicking bikes and lawnmowers.'

'But Gemma, what are we gonna do with all that cash?'

'Burn it. It's trouble and it's worthless.'

'Perhaps we could still make it across to France …'

'It's pounds, had you exchanged it for euros we could have gone. We'll stay here and see what happens …'

'We finally get some money together and they go and ban it – just my luck.'

'You haven't been following what's been going on over the past year. A revolution has taken place – there is no government, no Conservatives or Labour. The people are running the country; me and you are the government. I've been showing you the app but you're not interested.'

'I'm not interested in all that politics and stuff. I can't read, can I? No one's gonna want a stupid git like me in their government when I can't even read. What use am I, apart from washing cars down at the yard and nicking bikes?'

'You are good at judo.'

'I don't have time for judo, you know that.'

'Get a shower, we'll go to the town hall and talk to someone.'

Gemma dumped the carrier bag of used bank notes in a builder's skip. At the town hall they talked to Norman, a former estate agent, now a consultant engaged to help people redeploy.

'Just to remind you, I'm here as a kind of sounding board, in this new government we are all the same – well, we're not all the same – we are all very different, but we try to help each other as best we can. And I'm new to this as you can probably tell. Everything is new. This is my first time interviewing. I see by your ages that you are voters.'

'What?' said Oscar.

'He don't know nothin' about it, Norman. I've been trying to explain but he's not interested.'

'That's okay, there's plenty of time to pick it up. Tell me about yourselves.'

'I work at Tesco and Oscar here works at the car wash, you know. Handwash Extraordinaire down at the corner. But I reckon he can do better than that. He's a black belt in judo.'

'2nd Dan,' said Oscar, staring at the ceiling.

'Have you ever coached judo?' asked Norman.

'Yeah, of course, with judo it is mainly coaching. Everyone coaches the lower grades; that's the great part of it.' Oscar stood and took hold of an imaginary opponent. 'A brown belt will be fighting with a blue belt, say, and he'll notice a weakness in the kid's technique. So, he'll stop and put him right – *step in close and draw your feet together with your knees bent, then turn and straighten your legs at the same time pulling him across your hip –* come this side of the desk Norman and I'll show you.'

Norman politely declined Oscar's well-intentioned offer of a judo lesson and turned to Gemma. 'Gemma, are you happy to continue at Tesco?'

'Yeah, I'm on the checkout so nothing much has changed – well, there's no cash – it's all shopping cards now. I fill up shelves and push the Hoover around when it's slack, but it's early days and if it gets too boring, I'll apply to retrain as a brain surgeon.'

'Don't joke,' he turned to Oscar. 'What else are you good at?'

'Nothing, I can't read or write. I had special lessons at school but they couldn't do anything.'

'Are you happy in your flat?' Norman looked at their address.

'It's a bit damp in places, there's mould, and the window frames are rotten,' said Gemma.

'It needs pulling down if you ask me,' added Oscar.

Norman: 'I don't know the building. I'll note the address for a surveyor to swing by and take a look. Oscar, the country needs builders, is that something you might consider a possibility?'

The discussion continued and Oscar and Gemma were booked on to a two-day course designed to assess their innate skills, abilities and ambitions.

*

On the app: 'Please help if you can; we are working towards easing the bottleneck in NHS rehabilitation. If you know of a venue that can be easily converted to one-person units let us know. It could be a public building or disused offices – use your imagination. We need a twenty-four-hour rota of volunteers who can look after recovering patients until they are well enough to go home. Also – professional nurses (perhaps retired nurses) to administer medicine and change dressings, etc. The volunteers will act as carers who will cook food, serve it or feed it to the patients, liaise with relatives and so on.'

*

On the app: 'Fishermen (anglers) wanted to monitor river pollution. You will be required to take samples of river water whenever you go fishing. The more often the better, but once a week is fine. There is a specific app for your local river where you'll find all the information. It's not only fishermen, kids are keen to help with this kind of project and schools are getting involved. As soon as we find the source of any pollution we will put a stop to it. We have the power, ha ha!'

George

Pre-revolution George was comfortably off and never wanted for anything material. A widower, he now lives alone in the family house overlooking the heath. In the days of housing markets, with its six bedrooms, three bathrooms, sauna and heated swimming pool it had boasted a price tag of around five million pounds. George is eighty, a former banker who was quite reconciled to the revolution. He had voted for it. George knew all too well the vacuous nature of money and its disproportionate dominance over life and the planet.

He had a son in America who was also in banking and a daughter in Yorkshire who visited once or twice a year. His daughter had married young and although George's wife had disapproved, George reckoned that, providing the young couple were happy, it was no business of theirs.

He helped them with a deposit on a house and, to be fair to his son, had shipped him a Lowry and a Pissarro as soon as he realised they would soon be unsellable in Britain.

Two brothers used to cut the grass and keep the garden tidy but they had stopped coming, the cleaning lady and her daughter had also stopped coming, as did the window cleaner. They all stopped coming as soon it became clear that money – the reason they came – was about to disappear. So, the autumn of 2022 saw the grass grow tall and the weeds outgrow the perennials. The mixed beds developed into mixed beds of cultivated hybrids and rampant weeds. The greenhouse became impenetrable; panes cracked, glass fell in allowing the winds to howl through and dislodge the door which flapped on its runners until that glass smashed, too.

In the house, dust settled and stayed. Spiders occupied dark corners and their intricately woven webs collected more dust.

Shortly after Day Zero, there was a knock on the door. *Well, they can't be selling anything* … George opened it.

There was a young couple, a man and wife, so George invited them into the living room.

'I'm Cedric and this is Wilma. We just want to know if you are okay and if you need any help. Shopping – although it isn't really shopping any more – the garden or cleaning.' Cedric might easily have drawn a finger through the dust.

'Also,' said Wilma, 'we would like to know if there is anything you would like to do to help society. You are aware of the new government, aren't you?'

'I am, my dear, I most certainly am. I am a sixty-seven-millionth of said government and a voter, to boot.' He snapped his fingers victoriously. 'I would like a cleaner to come regularly, the garden needs looking after – especially the greenhouse and the windows need cleaning. I'm not so quick on my feet any more and my balance is poor.'

'How about shopping?'

'That seems to work as before. I phone the supermarket and the goods are delivered, they swipe my shopping card in their little contraption and off they go. As for my contributions to society – I feel it would be right for me to move out of this big house. It's a family house and not suitable for an old man like me. I need a smaller place, perhaps a flat – although the prospect of noisy neighbours worries me a bit. What do you think?'

Wilma: 'We'll get a housing adviser to come and visit you. There are lots of choices – a flat, as you mentioned – managed accommodation where there are in-house medics and a clinic – and then there are retirement villages which are also regularly visited by doctors and nurses.'

'Or you can stay here,' said Cedric. 'There's no rush, we'll find you a cleaner and a gardener and make sure the windows are cleaned.'

'The garden isn't so urgent, but spring is just around the corner and the long grass is lying flat. The lawn will need sprucing up – a couple of early cuts should do the trick.'

George was pleased with the visit. Cedric and Wilma were sympathetic without being condescending. He put the television on – most of the channels had gone. There were no commercial channels of course, and the BBC had new management. Much of the home news was about app activity; George had to admit that he found so much information difficult to digest. There were a couple of film channels and he was about to select a film when the phone rang, it was his son Vincent, phoning from America.

'Hi Dad, we're coming home.'

Vincent had moved to the USA in 2005 before the financial crash of 2008. In 2007, he met his wife. Life was good and now they had twin girls aged five.

Vincent: 'The news channels over here hardly report on what's happening back home, but I can see via the Internet that the revolution is going to be a success.'

George: 'The revolution has taken place, it's early days, and we won't know if it's a success for about another fifty years. But hopes are high.'

Vincent: 'Are there any restrictions on people returning from abroad?'

George: 'No, no, I don't think so, I'll find out. But that's a big decision – and so sudden – and I'm glad – but why?'

Vincent: 'Money is dead. The revolution will spread, I'm sure of it. And when it hits America, it won't be peaceful – it could get nasty. I could stay and chance it, but I want to raise my kids in the country that slayed the dragon. Can we stay with you until we find somewhere to live?'

George: 'Yes, of course, nothing would please me more. But do you really think the revolution will spread as far as America?

Vincent: 'Dad, money is dead and without money, capitalism can't exist. And without capitalism, America can't exist, at least not in its present form. I'll be in touch.'

Fielding, Mullard and Davies

At a small accounting firm, the senior partner, Mr Davies, addressed his colleagues. No one knew what the future held; accountancy had no place in a moneyless economy. The company would close, or be mothballed, as Mr Davies liked to think of it. He had taken over from his father and had reckoned on another thirty years developing the partnership. Those ambitions were in the bin – now he had to rethink the rest of his life and that of the partnership, too. Cake, tea and coffee were served to rally the troops for the big wind-down.

Davies: 'Thank you for turning up, these are our last days together and you are not obliged to be here. The projects you are working on need to be balanced and finalised as year-end accounts. This might seem pointless but let's be professional. There will be no pay at the end of the month, so those who want to leave now, please feel free.'

Fielding: 'Need this be the end of working together?'

Brian the Bookkeeper: 'Yeah, that's right; the revolution might fizzle out and in a couple of months we'll be back picking up the pieces.'

Fielding: 'Maybe, but I somehow don't think so and that's not what I meant; the revolution won't fizzle out, it's here to stay. It just seems a pity not use our accountancy skills and the office infrastructure to help our new government. We can't count money; but there must be a demand for our organisational skills. Money has gone but the economy remains and unless this new economy is managed efficiently, there will be lots of waste. Man-hours must balance against work to be done. Those who have lost their jobs need new careers – it has to be organised.'

Secretary: 'How do you mean exactly?'

Fielding: 'Take, for example tax inspectors; HM Revenue and Customs alone employs over sixty-six thousand people. In *A World without Money and Politicians*, it's estimated that around a third of all workers are employed solely in and around money – counting it – collecting it and so on. A third of the workforce is around ten million people. That's a lot of workers. Unless their redeployment is managed carefully, there could be a lot of waste, including people moving abroad.'

Felicity: 'Spread them around and that would mean a shorter working week.'

Fielding: 'And filling the gaps that exist in essential services. There are massive shortages in the building industry – NHS – agriculture and so on.'

Mullard: 'And factory workers, lorry drivers, labourers – people in jobs with demands on their physicality often work too hard resulting in wear and tear. Those workers should work fewer hours – don't you think? There needs to be a system that will regulate working hours so that it's fair for everyone.'

Felicity: 'Yeah, it would be fun to see Boris digging up the roads.'

Fielding: 'And in farming and food production, for example much of agriculture is highly automated, satnavs steering tractors – you must have seen the documentaries. Clever stuff indeed, but come harvest time there'll be demand for hands on the ground and nimble fingers picking blackcurrants.'

Felicity: 'No more foreign workers – no money.'

Fielding: 'Precisely, but we have our own workers and it needn't be three or four months sweating in the fields cutting broccoli – two or three weeks on a rota perhaps – I don't have the answer here and now – but it needs to be organised; like I said "man-hours matching work to be done".'

Felicity: 'A bit like the Kent hop pickers.'

Mullard: 'Interesting, Scout huts and a holiday atmosphere celebrating harvest time. Only the other day I was party to a conversation with some of my neighbours. We threw around the idea of growing veg in the gardens and sharing it. Some of us have greenhouses and we reckoned that we could grow enough to be self-sufficient and give some away to those living in flats or unable to "dig for victory".'

Fielding: 'Precisely, one garden growing root crops and another growing brassica; crop rotation on a small scale, and there are bound to be some farmers willing to offer advice.'

Secretary: 'It all needs coordinating – green fingers and spreadsheets.'

Davies: 'And it isn't only small-scale gardening, the whole of agriculture needs reviewing in the same way.'

Mullard: 'With the emphasis on avoiding waste, one would hope. Price is non-existent in the traditional sense. But you don't need to throw away an apple because of a few spots – eat it with a knife, and compost the spots.'

Felicity: 'Won't that make spotty compost?'

Brian the Bookkeeper: 'I'm off! I wish you all the best and thanks for the cake, but this isn't for me. I'm moving to the States.'

Davies: 'Do you have a job?'

Brian the Bookkeeper: 'Yes, I have a cousin in a firm of accountants in California. I'll be thinking of you and your spotty compost spreadsheets.'

Davies: 'Compost or cash – what's the difference?'

Brian: 'Look, I have enjoyed my time with the firm and don't want to leave on a sour note, but if you swallow all this communist bullshit and the so-called people's government … well you deserve what's coming to you.'

Davies: 'It's a fair way to run the country. Perhaps you prefer Boris or Liz Truss? Trump or Putin? You must see the futility of the constant call for growth? But it's up to you.'

Brian: 'It's not "a fair way of governing the country" because it's not true. It'll never work. Imagine trying to run this office without a management structure and strong leadership – it would be total chaos. The 'app' is a fake; there's some communist mastermind behind it – it might even be Putin pulling the strings.'

Mullard: 'Putin is not a communist. He is a capitalist dictator; he won't be following Britain's lead anytime soon. But good luck in California, send us a postcard.'

Brian: 'Don't trivialise what I'm doing. I'm giving up my house; I can't sell it because it's been stolen from me by the communist regime. I will arrive in the States penniless with a wife and kid – how easy do you think that will be?'

Davies: 'Strictly speaking, you owned your house jointly with the bank. But you still have full rights to live there, no mortgage to pay – and if the roof leaks, or you need a plumber – you don't have to pay for those services.'

Brian: '*If* the roofer turns up, and how long am I going to wait for a plumber? You're fools if you believe this is going to work. Online voting – *the app* – ha, it's rigged, can't you see it? No one in their right mind voted for it – I don't know anyone who voted for it.'

Davies: 'I voted for it. My father, the founder of this firm voted for it. And do you know what he said? That he'd spent all of his working life counting money, and why? Tidiness, order, perfect balance, and just so that our clients paid less tax, meaning less money for schools and hospitals.'

Brian: 'And he made money, don't forget that, and he lives well on a big pension – *money* – plays golf – which costs *money* – four or five holidays a year – more *money*. That's what money can do, that's why I want money. And just wait until your father realises all those privileges are over. See how he feels about "the people's government" then. I need to be in control of my life. If you seriously believe that coordinated compost bins and happy allotments can replace the complex business of running the United Kingdom then you deserve all that's coming to you. Goodbye.' Brian the bookkeeper walked out.

Davies: 'He doesn't understand.'

Felicity: 'He sees things differently.'

Davies: 'Those things he mentioned, playing golf and the holidays, they will be available to everyone now.

Mullard: 'We are the product of our education. Prep school, junior school, grammar school, college or university – but sewn into the seams of the school uniforms is the brainwashing … suppress the child and reprogramme it, twist it and produce a machine that will earn money and pay taxes.'

Felicity: 'Pink Floyd's *The Wall*, the conveyor belt, the sausage machine – they got it right.'

Mullard: 'And I think the people of this country have got it right – have you seen that we've sent some Russians their own app? That'll delight Putin!'

'Felicity: 'He's banned it. It's the biggest ever threat to his power. It would be the end of him … and his war. I'll make another pot of tea.'

*

'Is there going to be any kind of monitoring of what people do?' asked the cleaner. 'It's a shirker's paradise. Get up at 11 o'clock, roll down the pub for free lunch and beer, home again for an afternoon kip, free fish and chips and more beer all evening.'

Mullard: 'There have always been such people, a lifestyle funded by benefits and petty crime, but ask the app and see what reaction you get. I have a notion that behaviour will be down to the individual. Freedom also means freedom to be a slob. An individual's behaviour is dependent on the tolerance of others, and the occasional poke in the ribs from one's fellow citizens won't come amiss. Under the old regime behaviour was very much dictated by TV and advertising.'

Davies: 'When you think about it we never really decided our own behaviour and yes, it will take time to adjust. Perhaps after a few years things will fall into place for that sort of person.'

Secretary: 'Yeah, or they'll drink themselves to death. Couldn't we put together an accounting system whereby a person's contributions to society are balanced against how much they take from society? Debit and credit but without the money.'

Fielding: 'I think that would be the first step to reintroducing money – or "Big Brother is watching". And what's wrong with leaving it to chance? Isn't that how life should be? Isn't that the way the privileged classes have always had it? Wake up mid-morning, brunch at the golf club, a round of golf, home for a nap and an evening of sipping cocktails at some exclusive bar. Not so different from your fish and chips – cirrhosis-of-the-liver candidates.'

*

App modification

The app was constantly developing and needed some tweaking. Parliamentarians could now grade the comments of others –

1. Fast-track – 2. Requires expert guidance – 3. Non-starter.

Those marked *Fast-track* attracted the most comment and these were earmarked for debate at live parliamentary sessions.

Requires expert guidance – cases of river and sea pollution, for example, which clearly needed experts. Citizens' assemblies would be employed here with sewage, drain and water purification specialists on hand.

Non-starters – (four-year-old Mary and her request for more ice cream) were saved in a file and were available for perusal by anyone at any time.

Accountability – each comment on the app had to be traceable to its author and so had to be signed-off with full name and NI number. Entries without these details would be deleted.

*

Sustainable designs

Fast-tracked on the app: 'I have some designs for sustainable, repairable kettles and need a manufacturer willing to make them.' Several inventors had posted similar suggestions, and they were invited to attend exhibitions around the country with integrated workshops where they could present their inventions to manufacturers.

These 'Inventors' Conventions' were open to the public. Ideas were pooled. Patent rights were waived. These products were for the benefit of society rather than for making a fortune – which they certainly wouldn't have pre-revolution – they lacked the critical *planned obsolescence*.

*

Freedom of worship
Fast-tracked on the app: 'Now that we have freedom of speech I would like to raise a prickly subject; Islam in Britain. A report on the Manchester bombing eked out an apology from the head of MI5 for having allowed the perpetrator, who was in their sights, to slip through the net. It seems that there are thousands of these characters mingling freely among us. They live a double life of respectability and extreme Islam. To monitor these people 24/7 would take a rota of seven or eight per suspect – so perhaps tens of thousands of police officers. That can't be done (even today, when there is no financial cost) nor should it have to be done. Islam is incompatible with other religions and a medieval carbuncle on the twenty-first century. In my opinion, no religion is superior to any other (all organised religion is a waste of time if you ask me, it exploits human spirituality) but strict Islam doesn't fit comfortably with our Western culture. What is the answer? I honestly don't know. Ban all religion? – I don't think so. Ban Islam? That wouldn't be fair; there are too many good Muslims. I have some Muslim mates who I drink with down the pub and they take religion with a pinch of salt. Our people-led UK government sets fairness high on its list of principles but it's also fair that the citizens of the UK (of all religions) can go about their business free of terror.

'Under direct democracy, the frustration that forces terrorists into acts of violence no longer exists. Each person is empowered. If an extreme Muslim wants sharia law, if he wants to prevent girls from having an education – he has the freedom to argue his case on the app – just as I am now. And if those ideas are rejected – he must accept the decision of the majority or leave the country, or drop his religion or move to somewhere where those laws already exist.

'Radicalised extremists don't have a balanced view of freedom (of life, if you ask me). The religious dogma that rules them has erased (or forbids) the capacity for independent thought.'

Response to the above posting:

Parliamentarian: 'Who enforces the decisions that parliament makes? Say, after a long and thorough debate it's decided that Islam should be banned from the UK (extreme, and unlikely but stay with me). How, and who will round up the Muslims and deport them? Where will they be deported to? Who will demolish the mosques?'

Parliamentarian: 'What a terrible thought. It stinks of ethnic cleansing and that isn't what I voted for. I think we need to include Muslims in the debate – just as there is the Archbishop of Canterbury and the Pope as leaders of Christians, there needs to be a spokesman (or woman) to represent Muslims in Britain.'

Parliamentarian: 'Are there such Sikh or Buddhist heads of religion?'

Parliamentarian: 'Those religions are not known for acts of terror.'

Parliamentarian: 'I have no time for religion. It shifts responsibility of actions and thoughts from the individual to an imaginary god. And when it comes to terrorism and religion – look what the Christian Nazis did to the Jews in Hitler's Germany!'

Parliamentarian: 'But that atrocity wasn't committed in the name of Christianity. You are getting your lines crossed.'

Parliamentarian: 'No, but the persecution and genocide of the Jews was fundamental to Hitler's rise to power.'

Parliamentarian: 'Looking rationally at the broader picture, Islam is a significant problem, and it forces our new government's hand. Earlier governments swept such unpalatable subjects under the carpet, or to use the modern terminology – kicked the can down the road. Any imminent election took priority over engaging in an unwinnable fracas and upsetting a stroppy minority.'

Parliamentarian: 'The matter needs to be worked through using a series of citizens' assemblies with imams as experts.'

Parliamentarian: 'That won't work; all they'll do is quote the Koran at you all day.'

Parliamentarian: 'Muslims insist that the Koran is the word of God, unlike the Bible which was written by men. So anyone criticising the Koran is going against the word of God and therefore should be executed.'

Parliamentarian: 'We never had all these problems under the old traditional form of government.'

Parliamentarian: 'We did. And politicians did what politicians do – they played politics, as an earlier parliamentarian said, "kicked the can down the road". To address conflicts between religious groups would have meant upsetting the voters – so create a think-tank and forget about it until after the election. That is what I like about the new regime, we are in charge, there are no excuses, there are no politicians and no pussy-footing around – if there is an issue to be dealt with, it should be addressed immediately. The proverbial *can* always turns out to be a *can of worms* and now we have to find a solution.'

Parliamentarian: 'Yeah, *can* or *can't*.'

Parliamentarian: 'Most deeply religious people of any sect will prioritise the dogma of their faith over the law of the land.'

Parliamentarian: 'And that is fine when there is no threat to the public. Not many people in Britain are deeply religious and it seems that it's only Islamic fundamentalists who cross the line. We are probably talking about a few thousand people. If you move to a country, or live in a country you should be flexible and respect the customs and laws of the host nation.'

Parliamentarian: 'It should be recognised that not all problems have solutions. Each religion believes that their God is the one and only God, and that He (most Gods seem to be male) is the key to everlasting salvation. All the debating in the world won't change this.'

Parliamentarian: 'That isn't the point of the debate. Freedom of worship is desirable in any society – but so is freedom from terrorism. Twenty-two people were killed at the Manchester Arena bombing and over a thousand injured. We want our kids to be able to attend a concert without the fear of being murdered. We want to be able to walk the streets and return home with our heads on our shoulders. At least that's what I want for my family.'

Lucy and Nicola

One Friday evening, on their way home from birdwatching in the park, two retired women, Lucy and Nicola, called in at a pub to use the facilities. Some guys playing darts made them a pot of tea and showed them to the selection of home-made cakes. 'I can recommend the scones, my missis made them,' one of them said slapping his stomach, a trophy not to be proud of. 'There's jam and whipped cream in the fridge, good for the heart, be warned.'

*

Lucy and Nicola had been introduced to each other by interviewers of the type mentioned earlier. They were both widows who were having difficulties getting to grips with the new way of life. They hit it off and Lucy fell under the influence of Nicola's interest in birdwatching.

Lucy was intrigued by Nicola's eventful life; two husbands and five children. Nicola and her first husband had lived in Zimbabwe (where she took up rugby) and she only returned to England when he was killed by a charging elephant. Her second husband was a cordon bleu chef at top London restaurant – until he died after eating a poison mushroom – 'he was testing it before serving it up, very dedicated to his work, my second husband,' Nicola had said.

Lucy had had just the one husband whom she cared for until he eventually died of Alzheimer's. Their only son had irritatingly moved to Australia.

*

'Fancy a game of darts, love?'

'In a minute, when we've finished our tea and scones,' said Lucy.

'Can you play darts?' whispered Nicola.

'No,' giggled Lucy.

'I can, we'll whip their arses, just wait and see.'

They'd had no intention of playing darts, or having tea and scones, they had popped into the pub to use the loo and go home to Nicola's to record the birds they had spotted.

After the tea, and with a glass of wine, they entered the world of darts. The wine focused their aim and darts rebounding off the wire got them jumping.

'What's with the binoculars?'

'We've been birdwatching in the park.'

'Oh nice; seen anything interesting?'

'Birds are interesting per se – you probably mean, "did you see any rare birds?" Well, we may have done.' Nicola showed them the footage on her mobile.

*

The hastily recruited safety net of social workers halted Lucy's fall into depression. She was living in a house full of memories but empty of life. As soon as her son got a whiff of the realities of a moneyless economy in Britain, he moved to Australia to be near his wife's family, which was fair enough, Lucy reluctantly rationalised.

But her sadness had deeper roots. The removal of money meant there would be nothing for him to inherit on her death. She had always thought that her son loved her, and he did. *Love is difficult to measure and of course he must put his family first*. None of this was ever spoken about. But she knew, and her son knew that she knew.

And now she was speaking about it to strangers. The people interviewing Lucy listened carefully and probed deeper. 'Is there anything else you'd like to tell us?'

There was. Neighbours used to bring cakes and do bits of shopping. They'd bring flowers and arrange them in vases. Another used to do odd jobs about the house and always refused payment. 'I had imagined it was kind-heartedness, but as soon as they realised they'd not receive a penny when I died, they stopped coming.'

'We are compiling data on this precise feature of the revolution. It is an aspect of a money-based economy which needs understanding. Certain acts of kindness were clearly not entirely altruistic. Those, like you, with estates worth inheriting were treated kindly – in the hope of being remembered in the will. We are not talking about anything illegal or even immoral – *if we are going to be kind to someone, it might just as well be a rich person*. Our perception of each other is – or was – based on status and status was, to a greater or lesser degree, very much dependant on wealth. And now there is no wealth – not in the original sense. It will be intriguing to see how our values and our perception of each other change as the new regime gathers momentum – especially after a generation or two. We are collating the experiences of people in similar circumstances to yours, and there will be reports published when they are concluded.'

'Yes, that's interesting – about status I mean – perhaps qualities such as kindness, wit and basic honesty will be the new measure.'

'It could be; what an interesting observation. Do you have any questions?'

'Yes, what about charities?' asked Lucy.

'Charities?'

'Well, I used to donate to several charities, and now they don't exist. Like you, I'm interested in the more hidden aspects of money and its influence on us.'

'Charities did a lot of good – often in areas where the state failed. But registered charities had all the overheads of a conventional business – employees' salaries, rent, advertising and accountants, that sort of thing. Donations had to cover these costs before saving a single abandoned kitten.'

Lucy brewed a fresh pot of tea and replenished the biscuits. The social workers arranged for a health visitor and a builder to call – they also asked what Lucy, as a parliamentarian and citizen, could contribute to the country.

'Well, I've been expecting you to ask that. I'm a nurse, a state-registered nurse, I'm seventy next year and quite fit, I'm sure I could help out in the hospitals – perhaps not full-time, though.'

A builder repaired the flashings on the chimney stack and Lucy was taken up on her offer, she helped out at the hospital three mornings a week. She was also put in touch with Nicola and they hit it off. When she wasn't working at the hospital, she was birdwatching and they both joined the pub darts team.

*

21 January 2023
At the Albert pub the television held the drinkers' attention. The BBC news focused on the economy in Europe. 'In France protesters are fighting Macron's plans to increase the retirement age while the rest of Europe struggles with inflation, which currently stands at 10.4 per cent …'

Baldy: 'So what's the inflation rate in Britain?'

Stick, who hadn't noticed the smug grin spreading over Baldy's face: 'We ain't got no inflation you – oh, ha ha – yeah, nice one Baldy – makes you feel good don't it.'

Treasure: 'It really is amazing and, yes, imports will be more expensive but the strong gold price continues to bolster the pound. And as we become increasingly self-sufficient, we will import fewer goods.'

Aristotle: 'And the quality of our exports, especially the sustainable electrical goods, will certainly help the balance of payments.'

'Do you know something?' said Baldy, 'I feel genuinely happy. I'm proud of our country and what we've done.'

'Ahhhhhh …'

Aristotle: 'Enjoy the moment, Baldy, we've got a long way to go before we reverse all those centuries of shit politics.'

Lordy: 'Yeah, what's your take on this religion business – Islam and all that kerfuffle … hang on, turn up the volume.'

BBC: 'And now some app news – there is a growing demand for live parliaments to debate the "freedom of faith" issues. It is suggested that all parliamentarians go onto to the app to agree an agenda and date.'

Lee was already on the app, 'Ha, listen to these suggestions for the agenda; the freedom of Muslim women, radicalisation in prisons, circumcision of healthy infants (male and female), acknowledgement of UK law over religious dogma, the burning and mutilation of religious books ….'

Lordy: 'And it ain't even fireworks night!'

Stick: 'It soon will be.'

*

Live parliaments, 16 February 2023

Three hundred and seventy live parliaments, one agenda.

Due to the heavy load of business, it was agreed to hold live parliaments every Thursday until the backlog was cleared. Debate continued online and live parliaments served as witness that direct democracy was 'seen to be done'. Much of the agenda listed below had been chewed over online and required only a little fine tuning before being voted on.

This was the agenda to be worked through over next month or so:

The election of a permanent Chair for each parliament and a more regulated structure of parliaments.

1. How many parliaments and how many delegates per session?

2. Should their location be fixed?

3. Should each county have a dedicated app with their separate local parliaments focusing on local matters – schools, transport, emergency services, etc.? Local county councils are running these services, just as before, so there will be little or no disruption.

Defence

Online debate overwhelmingly supported the idea that there should be no radical change to the structure of Britain's defence systems. At some time in the future 'The International Emergency Rescue Force' would be established. This would be on standby 24/7 in case of catastrophes – earthquakes, floods and fires – mostly abroad, one would think (see *A World without Money or Politicians*).

Conscription

There was much talk about this and yet no definitive model had been decided. The suggestions varied between a six-month holiday camp and its original format – a two-year stint in the armed forces. It would most likely end up with five or six different options to suit all young men and women.

Prisons review

1. Should those held in prisons for crimes which no longer posed a threat be released? The drugs industry is dead. Theft was pointless – yes, items would be stolen but, it was thought, less so than before. It had been floated online that it was safe to release some prisoners and provide them with support and a restart plan.

2. Was it too soon to think about closing some prisons?

Shopping cards

The shopping card system was pointless unless a system of checking was introduced. How would gross or irregular patterns of consumption be overseen without flagging up *Orwell alarms*?

A panel in each county had already been set up to randomly check what people were taking from the supermarkets. The monitors would be changed yearly meaning that, over time, everyone would have a chance to be a shopping card monitor. However, checkout assistants – being parliamentarians – did a pretty good job of curbing overindulgent or wasteful customers.

'Three celery heads?'

'A dozen bottles of Chardonnay? You had a party last week, I recall.'

'All that cake will make you ill.'

More Nanny than Big Brother; nor was it very efficient, the customer could easily try another supermarket. But those who gorged on celery or punished their liver with white wine were, after all, entitled to do so.

Agriculture and pollution – sewage

The pollution of rivers and seas by pesticide and artificial fertilizer run-off had to be tackled. Testing had already begun and local pollutants – often rogue farmers were being brought into line. Citizens' assemblies were planned with agriculture and environmental experts on hand.

Census of the population and identity cards

1. It was known that many people had left the country, but not how many. Nor was there a comprehensive list or forwarding details for these individuals and families.

2. There was a significant body of online opinion that argued for monetary compensation for those who'd left the country. This needed to be thrashed out.

3. A by-product of processing 'foreign visitors' was a tightening up of the borders.

4. It was thought that many illegal immigrants had left the country, meaning a dramatic fall in the population – boosting the argument for a census. It was felt important to know who was in the country and where they lived.

5. Should identity cards be introduced?

Health checks

It was felt an open debate around 'health checks' would lead to a series of citizens' assemblies. The NHS was not yet ready to take on the extra workload, but wide-ranging health checks would eventually prevent disease and free-up hospital beds long term.

HS2

The North/South rail link was now largely an environmental issue. Abort – continue – or modify?

Islam

What does Britain want? Should we live in the constant fear of terrorist attacks? Should there be a charter that all adult Muslims must sign a pledge stating their loyalty to British law over the Koran. Those who refuse to sign or overstep the charter must leave the country – forcibly if necessary. This legislation would address: the freedom of Muslim women, radicalisation in prisons, circumcision of healthy infants (male and female) and the burning and mutilation of religious books.

*

And so, every Thursday another set of parliaments with a fresh set of parliamentarians met to plough through the acres of mess left by half a century of myopic mismanagement.

On 1 March 2023 the people of the Republic of Ireland would debate and decide their future governance. The people of Poland, Greece, Mexico and Italy began their own journey along the path to freedom. Very few individuals around the world escaped having their curiosity awakened; and murmurings stirred where murmuring – or even independent thought – was a dangerous practice.

Conclusion

This is a work of fiction, and of course no such revolution took place or ever will; we British – we humans – are too easily manipulated by the establishment psychopaths.

The top puppeteers (the wealthy) control their marionettes (the politicians), they in turn pull the strings of society – the civil service –education – the armed forces – and police. All the while 'no strings attached' criminal gangs enjoy the rich pickings of those activities outlawed by the outlaws. The black economy feeds the mainstream economy and vice versa.

General elections will come and go; the main parties will debate, argue and, of course, politicians will tell whoppers and side-step journalistic probing. Conversations will be had – the wrong conversations.

It is pure madness to fight against the flood of freshly printed banknotes and the lie that is representative democracy. Despite everything written here, despite the stack of ledgers proving corruption at the very top, we will continue to eat the crumbs from the politicians' banqueting table. Governments will continue to print money – boom and bust will waltz merrily on into eternity. And when the economy needs an emergency boost – business moguls will give the nod and politicians will contrive to bring about war.

There is no shame. When a man boasts that his privileged position allows him to grab a woman's private parts – when the boast is recorded – when the recording is broadcast to the furthest corners of the planet and the same man goes on to become the most powerful man in the world – then something is wrong, dreadfully wrong.

Winston, in George Orwell's *Nineteen Eighty-Four* is reading *The Theory and Practice of Oligarchical Collectivism* – he lets the book rest then reads again the paragraph:

… he knew better than before that he was not mad. Being in a minority, even a minority of one, did not make you mad. There was truth and there was untruth, and if you clung to the truth even against the whole world, you were not mad.

Strangely enough, I have never really doubted my sanity (although you, dear reader, must have wondered sometimes). We are all a bit mad; and we catch the stupidity virus from time to time. But I am resolute when it comes to the sentiments expressed in this book and I will continue to argue the case until I am persuaded otherwise – or draw my last breath.

Timeline

Covid	2020, 2021 and 2022
Vladimir Putin invades Ukraine	24 February 2022
Prime Minister Boris Johnson resigns	7 July 2022
Liz Truss becomes prime minister	6 September 2022
Her Majesty The Queen dies	8 September 2022
Liz Truss resigns	25 October 2022
Rishi Sunak becomes prime minister	25 October 2022
Inaugural Parliament	4 January 2023
Second Parliament and Day Zero	18 January 2023
General Election	4 July 2024